You're invited to a

CREEPOVER®

The Ride of Your Life

written by P. J. Night

SIMON SPOTLIGHT

New York   London   Toronto   Sydney   New Delhi

If you purchased this book without a cover, you should be aware that this book is stolen property. It was reported as "unsold and destroyed" to the publisher, and neither the author nor the publisher has received any payment for this "stripped book."

This book is a work of fiction. Any references to historical events, real people, or real places are used fictitiously. Other names, characters, places, and events are products of the author's imagination, and any resemblance to actual events or places or persons, living or dead, is entirely coincidental.

SIMON SPOTLIGHT
An imprint of Simon & Schuster Children's Publishing Division
1230 Avenue of the Americas, New York, New York 10020
Copyright © 2014 by Simon & Schuster, Inc.
All rights reserved, including the right of reproduction in whole or in part in any form.
SIMON SPOTLIGHT and colophon are registered trademarks of Simon & Schuster, Inc.
YOU'RE INVITED TO A CREEPOVER is a registered trademark of Simon & Schuster, Inc.
Text by Ann Hodgman
For information about special discounts for bulk purchases, please contact Simon & Schuster Special Sales at 1-866-506-1949 or business@simonandschuster.com.
Manufactured in the United States of America 1114 OFF
10 9 8 7 6 5 4 3 2
ISBN 978-1-4424-9729-0
ISBN 978-1-4424-9730-6 (eBook)
Library of Congress Catalog Card Number 2013934700

PROLOGUE

An old Ferris wheel is a lonely sight at midnight.

Actually, this whole deserted fairground is a lonely sight. The wind tosses litter across empty paths that lead to empty rides. The dusty horses on the merry-go-round stand perfectly still. The faded signs at the concession stands brag about long-ago refreshments—ICED DRINKS! FRESH CARAMEL CORN!—but the windows are boarded up. No one will ever order anything again.

But somehow it's the Ferris wheel that looks the loneliest. Its lights were turned off years ago. Its cars sway uncertainly in the wind, their bolts and safety locks rusted away.

Wait. Is it really the wind that's moving those cars?

If you look more closely, is the wheel turning slowly, all by itself?

If you listen, is that a distant scream from the very top car?

Can't be.

Because this fairground is deserted. Remember?

CHAPTER 1

"I'm so, so, so, so sorry!"

Gabby Carter had just jumped out of her seat to hand her meal tray to the flight attendant, and she figured she would hand in her neighbor's tray as well. But leaning over made her tray table bounce into the air. Which had caused her drink to bounce into the air as well. Cranberry juice rained down the tray, dripping onto the floor and Gabby's armrest and the cover of the magazine that the woman in the seat next to her had been reading before she fell asleep.

"Sheesh. I just wanted to help without waking you up," Gabby said miserably.

"Well, you didn't," snapped the woman, who was all

tucked in for the flight. She had taken off her shoes and replaced them with woolen booties. She also had a sleep mask pushed up onto her head and a neck pillow resting on her collar. In other words, she didn't seem to care how crazy she looked. "I'm perfectly capable of turning in my meal tray by myself. And anyway, I wasn't sleeping."

"You were *too* sleeping!" Gabby protested. "I heard you sno—breathing deeply."

The woman glared at her. "I was resting my eyes. And I *needed* the rest, sitting next to you. Look at you. We practically just took off, and your seat already looks like a bird's nest. I can't believe they gave me a seat next to a child."

"We'll have everything back to normal in no time," said the flight attendant. He was a youngish man, and he looked as if nothing ever bothered him.

"Let's just clean up a little here," he said, "and we'll all be as good as new." From somewhere in his cart, he pulled out a damp towel and deftly began to mop up the spill. He glanced at Gabby. "Why don't you sit down and fasten your seat belt again?"

Gabby sat down. *An hour into the flight,* she thought, *and already I'm causing trouble.*

"And you, ma'am—would you like something else to read?" the flight attendant asked the woman next to Gabby.

"No!" she snapped. "Just take this away." She handed him the juice-stained magazine. Then she pulled a book of Sudoku and a pencil out of her purse and bent over the page with angry concentration.

"Is this your first flight?" the attendant asked Gabby.

Gabby sighed. "No. My sixth. And I've spilled something on every trip."

"Sometimes it's hard to sit still," the flight attendant said. "Anyway, I'm Toby." He gestured down at his name badge. "As I guess you already know."

"I'm Gabrielle," said Gabby. "Gabby for short."

"And where are you headed, Gabby? Besides Iowa, I mean."

"I'm going to visit my best friend, Sydney," Gabby told him more cheerfully. "She lives in a town called Trouble Slope. Have you heard of it?"

"I don't think so. Is it close to Des Moines?"

"It's, like, a two-hour drive.," said Gabby. "My aunt lives in Des Moines, so she's going to pick me up at the airport and drive me to Trouble Slope. It's a pretty small town. But it does have a college," she added. "That's where Sydney's parents work. They're both professors, and Trouble Slope was the only college they found that could hire both of them at the same time." She sighed. "So that's why they moved out of San Francisco a year ago."

To Gabby, it had felt like the longest year of her life. She had other friends, of course, but she and Sydney had been *best* friends since kindergarten. It hadn't been hard to stay in touch since Sydney had moved. The girls had texted or video-chatted pretty much every day. But texting and video-chatting were just not the same as having Sydney actually live in San Francisco.

"What's Sydney like?" Toby asked sympathetically.

"Sydney is—Sydney is *calm*," Gabby told him. "That's one of the best things about her. She never seems to worry or get flustered. She never leaves anything till the last minute. She's never late. She's the total opposite of me."

"Sounds as if you make a good team," Toby said. "She's calm, and you're—uh—energetic."

"Exactly! Sydney usually *likes* it when I do something crazy. Because she never would have thought of it."

"Well, I hope you have a—"

A voice suddenly broke in—the voice of the cranky woman next to Gabby, of course. "Don't you have anything to do besides stand here?" she asked Toby.

For a second, Toby looked startled. Then he arranged his face into a smile. "I'm sure I do," he said. "Thanks for the reminder. Can I get either of you anything before I go back to work?"

"You already asked me that," said Gabby's seatmate.

She is really *rude,* thought Gabby. It seemed as if the best thing she herself could do was not to give Toby any more trouble. "I'm fine," she told him. "But thanks for listening."

"My pleasure," said Toby. Then he leaned over and pointed at the cranky woman's Sudoku.

"That should be a five, not a three," he said. He winked at Gabby.

As Toby headed up the aisle, Gabby silently vowed that she would sit without moving for the rest of the flight. She wouldn't even use her half of the armrest. She would give her seatmate absolutely nothing to complain about. . . .

Gabby had been up late packing the night before.

Sitting motionless now, she felt her eyes starting to close. She had just one more thought before falling asleep.

I hope I don't end up leaning on that lady's shoulder.

"We're landing. Wake up!"

Once again the woman next to Gabby was making her presence known.

Gabby straightened up, rubbing her eyes. "We're landing?" she echoed in a blurry voice. "I slept for three hours?"

"Yes. You missed the movie. And the snack."

The woman's eyes rested on Gabby for a second. "I've been to Trouble Slope several times," she added abruptly. "I'm very well acquainted with that place."

Still groggy, Gabby struggled to sound polite. "You—you have? I mean, you are?"

"I had family there," said the woman. "They moved out as soon as they could."

"Is it a nice place?" Gabby felt stupid the minute the question was out.

"It certainly is not. It's dangerous."

"*Dangerous?*" Gabby echoed. She was wide awake now.

"That's what I said," the woman replied curtly. "It's especially dangerous for children. You'd be better off if you turned around and went home right now."

Before Gabby could answer, the plane touched down on the tarmac and came to a stop. Everyone started bustling around—including the woman next to Gabby, who jumped to her feet and pushed into the aisle ahead of all the other passengers.

Which was just as well, since Gabby hadn't come up with a response to her strange warning.

What a weirdo, Gabby thought as she reached down for her backpack.

Because—come on—how could a tiny town in the middle of nowhere possibly be dangerous?

Aunt Lisa spotted Gabby the minute she stepped into the baggage claim area. "Just look at you!" she marveled after giving her niece a hug. "I swear you've grown three feet since I saw you last. Are you hungry, by any chance? I know we're two hours ahead of California time, but—"

"I'm *starving,*" Gabby interrupted. "I feel like I ate lunch three days ago." She pulled out her phone to check the time. Seven o'clock. The plane had been right on schedule. And even though it was only five o'clock back at home, she was dying for supper.

"Let's eat here at the airport, then," said Aunt Lisa. "There won't be much besides fast food once we're out of Des Moines."

"It was really nice of you to pick me up, Aunt Lisa," Gabby remembered to say a few minutes later as she and her aunt studied their menus. They had found an airport restaurant, the Palm Palace, which was doing its best to persuade its customers that they were in sunny California. The tables were made out of surfboards, and a few pairs of flip-flops had been scattered around for realism.

"I was happy to pick you up!" replied her aunt. "I just wish I could see you for a real visit. If I didn't have this stupid work trip tomorrow, I'd keep you for a couple of days. I'm glad it's a two-hour drive to Trouble Slope so we can catch up."

"Aunt Lisa, have you ever heard anything . . . bad about Trouble Slope?" Gabby asked.

"Bad? What do you mean?"

"Well, this weird lady was sitting next to me on the plane, and she said it was dangerous there."

"Dangerous?" Aunt Lisa echoed. "A university town miles from any city? I'm guessing it's one of the safest places in the United States. What did this woman say, exactly?"

"Oh, she said a lot of stuff." Quickly Gabby ran through the story of her unfortunate encounter. "Spilling that juice was the most embarrassing moment of my whole life," she said.

Aunt Lisa gave a little cluck of irritation, but not because of Gabby. "That woman sounds awful. I'm sorry you had to spend the whole trip next to her."

Gabby giggled. "She was probably sorry she had to spend the whole trip next to me! Anyway, I'll stop thinking about it. Sydney would tell me there's no use worrying about stuff that's in the past. And I want to get into Sydney-mode before I see her. Oh, I can't wait!"

"Let's order dessert right away, then," Aunt Lisa suggested.

Gabby thought that would be a good idea.

"And now to remember where I parked my car," said Aunt Lisa when they had finished their ice cream (raspberry sorbet for Aunt Lisa, brownie batter for Gabby). "It's not always easy to spot—it's not that big."

That was an overstatement. Or was it an under-statement? Aunt Lisa turned out to have the tiniest car Gabby had ever seen—a green two-seater that looked about three inches tall. There was barely room for the two of them plus Gabby's backpack and suitcase, but after a short struggle, they managed to squeeze every-thing in. Aunt Lisa dug around in her purse until she found her parking receipt.

"Why bother waiting in line?" Gabby asked as they approached the ticket booth. "You could just drive under the cars ahead of us."

It was true that Aunt Lisa had to reach way, way up to hand the money to the parking-lot attendant.

"I hope you don't have a long way to go in that lunch box," he said as he passed back some change and a receipt.

"Just a couple of hours," said Aunt Lisa.

She edged the car forward, waiting for the mechani-cal arm to lift. "And . . . we're off!" she said to Gabby. "Soon you and Sydney will be together again."

CHAPTER 2

As soon as they'd reached the highway, Gabby asked her aunt if she knew how Trouble Slope had gotten its name.

"Maybe there was an avalanche or there was a fire or something. There must be some kind of legend behind it, don't you think?"

Aunt Lisa shook her head. "If there's anything bad connected with that name, I've never heard it."

"But why would people give a town that kind of name if it didn't have something the matter with it?" Gabby persisted.

"Honey, there are towns with weird names all over the United States," said Aunt Lisa. "Alabama has a town called Burnt Corn. There's a Toad Suck in Arkansas and a Buttermilk in Kansas. And a Hot Coffee, Mississippi, and a Texico, New Mexico, and—"

Gabby couldn't help interrupting. "Wait. How do you know all those names?"

"I had to memorize them for a trivia contest in college," Aunt Lisa told her. "But you get the point."

"I guess so." *Still, those towns got their names for a reason,* Gabby thought stubbornly. *And I bet Trouble Slope had a bad reason.*

She sighed as she looked out the passenger window. It was still light out, but there wasn't much to see—just flat farmland rolling by, and a house once in a while. "There's not a lot going on here, is there?" she asked.

"The farmers who live here would probably disagree with you," Aunt Lisa replied. "But it's not much of a landscape. I brought a couple of audiobooks if you'd like to listen to one. They're in my bag."

"That would be great," said Gabby. She rummaged through the choices and pulled out an audiobook called *Haunting Tales of Haunted Houses.* "Let's listen to this one. I love scary stories." She slid in the first CD.

A swirl of ominous music filled the car, and Gabby gave a happy sigh as she settled back to listen. After a

few minutes, though, she started to have trouble following the story.

Gabby didn't think of herself as a napper. Her parents had once told her that she'd stopped napping when
she was three months old. ("And we've never recovered,"
her dad said.) She had already fallen asleep on the air-
plane. On top of that, the first story on the CD was
about a headless woman who lived in a cabin near a
campground—not the kind of thing to make someone
sleepy. Nevertheless, Gabby's eyes kept closing as she
listened. After a little while, she gave in and fell asleep.

"'IT WAS THE HAND OF DOOM!'" thundered
the audiobook narrator, and Gabby sat up with a start.
Looking out the window, she saw that darkness had
fallen. Aunt Lisa's little car sped through the night,
alone on the road. There was a different story on the
CD now, something about a ghost ship.

"'Through the fog, a flickering light appeared,'" read
the narrator. "'The sailors leaned forward, straining to
see what lay ahead. . . .'"

At that same moment, Gabby saw a cluster of lights in
the distance. These lights weren't flickering, though—
they were sharp and bright.

"What's that over there, Aunt Lisa?" she asked. "Those lights out in the middle of nowhere?"

"'But from the crow's nest, the lookout called, "Turn back! For Pete's sake, turn back!"'" (That was the CD again.)

"The ghost lights?" said Aunt Lisa distractedly.

"No! Those real ones over there!"

Aunt Lisa glanced to see where Gabby was pointing. "Oh, over there. I think that's an abandoned fairground off the old highway," she said. Then she reached forward and turned up the sound a little.

Gabby could tell that her aunt was totally immersed in the story, so she decided to keep quiet until it was over. At least they were drawing closer to the lights—finally there would be something to see. She pressed her face to the glass as they reached the edge of the fairground.

"This fairground's not abandoned!" she blurted out, forgetting that she was trying not to talk. What could Aunt Lisa have meant before? The fairground looked busy and bright and pulsing with life. Cars filled with screaming kids were rocketing down an impossibly tall roller coaster. Nearby, a Tilt-A-Whirl spun crazily around. There seemed to be dozens of other rides, including a majestic, colorfully lit Ferris wheel that was just coming to a stop. And the fun house—Gabby gave a delighted shiver when she saw the huge, spooky face painted on the front. Half evil clown, half magician, the face seemed to be leering right at her. Above the face, in old-fashioned lettering, was a sign that read THE MAGIC FUN HOUSE OF CLAUDIUS THE MAGNIFICENT.

Now Gabby was too excited to stay quiet. "It's a real live fair!" she squealed. "Look, Aunt Lisa! The roller coaster is awesome! Do you think this fair is close to Sydney's house? Do you think her parents will let us come here? I've always wanted to go to a country fair! I wonder if there's a prize cow!"

Aunt Lisa wasn't looking at the fair. She was staring at the road ahead of her, but she looked confused.

"I . . . I'm not sure what you mean, Gabby. Are you talking about those run-down old rides over there in the cornfield?" She pointed at the bright lights of the carnival, which were getting smaller in the distance. "That place doesn't look like it's operated in years."

Now it was Gabby's turn to look confused. "But— no. It definitely isn't run-down. Maybe your eyes are tired? From all this driving?"

"Honey, we've only been on the road for about an hour and a half," said Aunt Lisa soothingly. "It's been a long day for you. Maybe the audiobook gave you bad dreams. Let's turn it off, shall we?" She punched the off button. "Listen—can you hear crickets?"

Gabby bit her lip and didn't answer. *I know I'm awake,* she thought. *And I know I was awake five minutes ago.*

She hadn't been dreaming then, and she wasn't dreaming now. Behind them, she could still see the tiny dots of light from the fairground. It had to be Aunt Lisa who was mixed up. Maybe she had been paying too much attention to the audiobook.

But before Gabby could say anything more, Aunt Lisa pointed to a sign on the side of the road.

"Look! Trouble Slope is the next exit. We're almost there!"

And ten minutes later, she was pulling into the driveway of a white Victorian house.

Before Gabby could get her seat belt unfastened, Sydney was rushing out of the house toward her. Gabby was so excited that she leaped out of the car and crashed right into Sydney, knocking both girls to the ground. For a split second they just blinked at each other as they lay sprawled on the grass. Then both of them clambered to their feet and began hugging and jumping up and down.

"Are you okay?" asked Gabby. Then she rushed on before Sydney could answer. "I can't believe how long your hair is! And you're so much taller!"

"And I love *your* hair braided like that! And *you're* . . . not really so much taller," said Sydney, laughing. Gabby had always been one of the shortest girls in their grade.

Light from the open front door was streaming out onto the dark lawn, and Gabby saw Sydney's parents watching from the doorway. "Hi, Mr. and Mrs. Costa!" she said excitedly. "I'm here! I'm really here!"

"You really are," said Mrs. Costa. "And we're so glad!" She turned toward Aunt Lisa, who had just walked up to the front steps. "You must be Gabby's aunt Lisa," she went on. "Come on in!"

"Yes! Come in!" echoed Gabby without thinking. "I mean, yes, let's go in. Oh, wait! My backpack and suitcase. Where are they? Are they here? I don't want to forget them."

"They haven't gone anywhere, honey. I'll bring them in for you," said Aunt Lisa. "You go on."

"Wow," said Gabby as soon as she stepped into the

Costas' front hall. "This is an actual country house. It's so different from your apartment, Syd!"

"Would you like to come into an actual room, Gabs, or would you like to stand in the hall?" inquired Sydney's father.

Gabby giggled. "I'd like to come into all the rooms at once," she said. "Oh, good—here's my stuff. Thanks, Aunt Lisa!"

"My pleasure." Aunt Lisa set Gabby's suitcase and backpack on the floor and reached out to shake hands with Sydney's parents. "It's so nice of you to invite Gabby to stay," she said. "As you can probably imagine, she was *extremely* eager to get here."

"Sydney's been the same way," Mr. Costa said. "Gabby, Gabby, Gabby, all day long. Anyway, let's all sit down. What can we get you travelers? Sydney forced us to buy most of the food in Iowa, so we've got anything you might want."

"I'd love a cup of coffee," said Aunt Lisa.

"Coffee? At this hour? You're not planning on driving home tonight, are you?" asked Sydney's mother. "We have the guest room all ready."

Gabby's aunt shook her head with a rueful smile. "I'd

love to stay, but I've got a business trip starting tomorrow morning. I need to head back. But coffee would definitely be a help."

"Don't worry, Aunt Lisa. That audiobook will keep you wide-awake for the drive," said Gabby. To Sydney, she said, "We listened to ghost stories all the way here."

"Gabby, *you* may not have coffee," said Sydney's father. "You may be tired, but somehow I bet that you and Sydney will still manage to stay up later than you should."

Mr. Costa was right. Long after they'd gotten into the twin beds in Sydney's large room, the two girls were still talking. And they were still talking long after Sydney's parents went to bed too. But now it was past midnight, and their energy was starting to flag. They kept yawning, and their sentences were getting farther and farther apart.

"There was something I wanted to ask you," Gabby said drowsily. "What was it?"

A pause. "What was what?" Sydney asked.

"What I wanted to ask"—Gabby gave an enormous yawn—"Ask. You."

"Okay," said Sydney.

"No. Wait. Oh!" Gabby sat up in bed. She had remembered what it was. "The fair. Can we go?"

Sydney rolled over onto her back. "What fair?" she asked after a few seconds.

"The one I passed when we were driving here. In the cornfield. You must have seen it before—it's so close!"

Sydney yawned. "We've already had the fair," she said in a blurry voice. "It was a couple of weeks ago. But it's not near here. It's almost an hour away."

"Syd, I saw a fair right before we got off the highway," Gabby protested. "There were all these lights, and lots of people, and a roller coaster and a Ferris wheel and—"

"I know what a fair is," Sydney interrupted. "And I know that there's no fair going on around here. You must have been dreaming."

It was the second time that night that someone had told Gabby she was dreaming. She was about to argue when she heard soft snores and realized that Sydney had fallen asleep for good.

Oh, well, she thought as she closed her eyes. *There is a fair near here—I know there is! And I'll prove it.*

But maybe, for now, it could wait. . . .

CHAPTER 3

"I'm telling you, Gabs, there's no fair! Can't we just eat our breakfast?" Sydney took a bite of cereal and returned to the article she was reading.

Gabby sighed. She had forgotten how long it took Sydney to wake up in the mornings. Sydney always needed a little while to check her e-mail and the news on her tablet—and she always needed a "sensible breakfast." Which, to Gabby, translated into a breakfast that took a long time to eat. Gabby, on the other hand, always started her mornings *ready*—ready for any activity and ready to talk about any topic that came up. Ready for anything except eating, that is. Her stomach never seemed to wake up until a couple of hours after she did.

So right now, Gabby was sitting at the dining room table, sipping a glass of milk and watching Sydney eat cereal, toast, and a smoothie made out of fruit, yogurt, and some kind of disgusting green powder.

"I swear, Syd, I saw one on the way here," she said. "And it looked like so much fun! I've never been to a real country fair. Don't you want to show me some of the wonderful things about living in the country? Things like fairs?"

Sydney put down her spoon and looked at Gabby, shaking her head. "You and your imagination," she said. "For the millionth time, the fair was *two weeks ago*. The volunteer firefighters put it on every year to raise money. It's really crowded—people come from all over the place—and it's really fun, but it's really gone now. When you come to visit next year, we'll make sure you're here at the same time as the fair. Okay?"

"No! I mean yes, I'd love to come next year, but no, you're wrong about *this* fair that I saw with my own two uncrazy eyes last night!"

Sydney's father had been taking some breakfast dishes into the kitchen and had come back into the dining room in time to hear the last bit of the girls' conversation. Now he was frowning slightly.

"You're actually half-right, Gabby," he said. "There is a fairground off the highway—if you were to walk through the cornfield behind our house for about half an hour, you'd get there."

"See, Sydney? I told you so," Gabby crowed.

"But," Mr. Costa said, "that fairground is definitely abandoned. Since the new highway was built, I bet no one's set foot there. It's not safe to poke around abandoned sites, and it's not legal to trespass, either."

Gabby could see his point—about the trespassing, at least. She didn't want to argue about what she'd seen the night before. It would be rude. So she smiled and told Mr. Costa that she'd forget about the fair.

"But I still think we should go check it out," she whispered to Sydney when Mr. Costa was out of the room.

"Shhhh! We can talk about it later," Sydney whispered back. Gabby took that as a good sign. At least Sydney wasn't ruling out the whole idea. . . .

"Girls, are you going to get dressed so we can go?" Sydney's mother called from upstairs. She had offered to take them to town so they could do some shopping and visit the campus where Sydney's parents taught.

"Okay, Mom," Sydney yelled back. "I'll just make a

smoothie for Gabby to bring along in the car." From the dozens of sleepovers they'd had, Sydney was familiar with Gabby's breakfast habits.

"Don't put in any of that green powder, whatever it is," Gabby said.

"But Gabs, it's a powdered superfood. It's really healthy!"

"I don't care if it's the healthiest powder on earth. I don't eat *green* in the morning. Just pink, orange, and white."

Sydney shook her head, smiling. "And you say *I'm* the one who's unadventurous."

Trouble Slope might have had a bad name, but it was a fantastic place to visit. Before she turned them loose, Mrs. Costa gave the girls a quick tour of the campus highlights. There was a ten-foot-tall prairie dog statue. A double-size hockey rink as well as a regulation-size one. ("The players practice on the double rink to increase their stamina," explained Mrs. Costa.) A working dairy where agriculture students made ice cream from the milk of cows they'd raised themselves.

"I'm starting to think I want to come here for college," said Gabby.

"Oh, I hope you do!" Mrs. Costa told her. "It would be fun to have you in one of my history classes. And speaking of classes, I've got to do a little work. Would you girls like to go into town now? I could pick you up in a couple of hours. Sydney, you know how to walk to town from here, right?"

For Gabby, it was a new experience being able to wander around wherever she and Sydney wanted. Back at home, her parents were just starting to allow her to use public transportation on her own. But in Trouble Slope, Sydney was allowed to walk or ride her bike pretty much anywhere. And since this was a college town, it had tons of great places to shop. The two girls went to a bead shop, two bookstores, a pottery place, and a tiny café that was famous for its cheesecakes.

"I wonder if people think we're college students," Gabby said as they ate their cheesecake at a little table outside.

"Probably not," said Sydney. "We look pretty much the age we are."

"Okay, Miss Unimaginative. Where do you want to go next?"

Sydney thought for a second. "There's a cool vintage shop the next street over. Let's try that."

The shop was named the Time Traveler. It was crammed with great stuff, and the grandfatherly man behind the counter didn't seem to mind how long they poked around. "Let me know if there's anything special you're looking for," he said with a smile before going back to his book.

There were strange old toys, like a doll that talked if you pulled the ring on her back. "And look how weird Barbies used to be," Sydney marveled. "Their eyes looked like seeds, and they didn't even have long hair!"

Gabby was examining an old game called Surprise Date. "Let's buy this, Syd," she said. She read aloud from the box. Behind the door is your dream date . . . or your total opposite! Will he be cute and ready for a ski date? Or will he be . . . a loser?'"

"Is that the guy who's supposed to be the loser?" Sydney asked, pointing. "Because I'd rather go on a date with him than the guy on the skis."

The man behind the counter chuckled. "They keep remaking that game," he said. "The one you've got there is from 1965. There's a later one with a snowboarding guy instead of a skier that I'm still trying to track down. I don't know if he's a date or a loser."

Gabby moved on to the clothing racks. "Do you have any vintage T-shirts?" she asked.

"Sure thing. See the pile in that corner, under the old chess table?"

There turned out to be tons of great old T-shirts, but most of them were too big for the girls to wear even as beach cover-ups. "I'd get this one, but it would come down past my knees," said Sydney mournfully. She held up a red shirt printed with different kinds of candy.

"These look like they're more our size," said Gabby, pulling out a box from under another table. A sleek black cat that must have been hiding behind the box darted out and hopped onto the counter. "Here's one with a Ferris wheel on it. And this one has a merry-go-round. Hey, wait a sec—these are *all* T-shirts about fairs!"

It was true. Each shirt in the box had a fair theme. And they all had the same bold lettering written on the back: CLAUDIUS THE MAGNIFICENT WELCOMES YOU.

"Whoa." Gabby's voice was almost a whisper. "Claudius the Magnificent is the guy I saw on the carnival sign last night."

"No way!"

"Yes. Yes! This *proves* I wasn't dreaming," said Gabby triumphantly. She turned to the sales clerk.

"Sir, is this fair around here?" She pointed to the words on the back of one shirt.

The clerk didn't look as cheerful as he had a few minutes before. "Used to be," he said shortly, slowly stroking the black cat's fur.

"Where was it?" asked Gabby.

"Off exit seventeen on the old highway," said the man. "It's not there anymore. And those fair T-shirts aren't for sale."

His smile was gone now. He picked up a folder and began going through the papers inside. He seemed, suddenly, very busy.

"They don't have the fair anymore, you mean?" asked Sydney.

"Right."

Gabby could see that the man didn't want to talk about the fair, but she was too interested to let it go. "When did they stop having it?" she asked.

"I'm not sure," said the clerk. "Some time ago."

"Well, why?"

Whack! The sales clerk slammed his folder against the counter. The cat didn't move a muscle, just stared coolly at Gabby and Sydney. "Look, are you two going to buy something or not?" he demanded. "Because if you don't want anything, maybe you could go bother someone else."

Gabby had actually been planning to buy the Surprise Date game, but now the thought of bringing it up to the counter seemed impossible. Together, she and Sydney walked quickly out of the store. The bell on the door gave a cheery ring as the door swung shut behind them.

"What was that about?" Gabby cried as soon as they were outside.

Sydney glanced back at the store. "I have no idea. We weren't doing anything wrong. Or do you think he got mad because we unfolded too many T-shirts?"

"Oh, come on," said Gabby. "In that kind of store, people rummage through everything. He was fine until I mentioned the fair."

"Why would he get mad about *that*?"

"I don't know," said Gabby. "But you've got to admit it, Sydney. There's something strange about that abandoned fairground." She bit her lip, thinking. "I wonder how we can find out more. There's got to be something online. . . ."

"Unfortunately, we're supposed to meet my mom in"—Sydney checked her phone—"eight minutes. Maybe we can do some research later."

"There's one thing we know for sure, though," said Gabby. "We know that there used to be a fair off the highway. Your father *and* the guy in the vintage store *and* my aunt all said it was abandoned—but I saw that fair last night. All brightly lit. Ferris wheel and all. Syd, you *can't* still think I dreamed it."

"I guess you didn't," said Sydney slowly. "It's weird, for sure. But I can't make the story fit. Why did you see lights if the fair is abandoned? And if it's *not* abandoned, why don't any grown-ups know that?"

"I can't figure that stuff out either," said Gabby. "There's only one thing to do. Don't you agree?"

"Go home and forget about it?" said Sydney hopefully.

"Syd, you sometimes make it hard to have an adventure," said Gabby. "But I know *you* know what we have to do . . . we have to visit that fairground ourselves."

CHAPTER 4

"This is like a forest," said Gabby. She swatted vigorously at a stalk of corn in front of her. "We're adventurers chopping our way through the jungle. We move silently forward as—"

But Sydney interrupted. "Stop! It's already enough of an adventure as it is! I mean, we lied to my parents, and now we're going to trespass at a—a forbidden fairground. I don't need anything more exciting than that."

"We didn't exactly lie to your parents," said Gabby. "We told them we wanted to take a walk before dinner. We just didn't tell them *where* we wanted to walk. And at breakfast, your father didn't say we couldn't go to the old fairground. All he said was 'It's not safe to poke around abandoned sites, and it's not legal to trespass, either.'"

Sydney was staring at her. "That *is* what he said. That's *exactly* what he said. How did you remember it all?"

"I taught myself to do it with my parents," Gabby told her. "Being able to repeat what they said word-for-word has gotten me out of a lot of trouble. Like let's say they accuse me of breaking some kind of rule—I can usually prove that they never set it up as an actual rule."

Sydney grimaced. "I don't think my parents will see it that way if they find out what we're doing."

"And *that*," said Gabby firmly, "is why we have to make sure they don't find out."

When they'd gotten home from their day downtown, Mrs. Costa had plunked herself down at her desk. "I have a ton of papers to grade," she'd told the girls. "You can take care of yourselves until supper, right?"

"Mom! Of course we can! We're not babies," Sydney had said indignantly. "We'll go for a walk until it's time to eat."

"Sounds great. We'll be eating at six thirty," said Mrs. Costa. "See you then."

That had been at about four thirty, so the girls

knew they had plenty of time. And it had been easy to walk into the cornfield behind the Costas' backyard: Mrs. Costa's desk faced the front yard.

Of course Gabby had seen cornfields, but she'd never been in one. It really did feel like a jungle—or an ocean. In front of her, behind her, to her left, and to her right, there was nothing to see but tall, tall stalks of corn.

"Syd, are you sure we're going in the right direction?" she asked.

"Yup. As long as we keep the sun on our right, we'll be fine. The fairground is south of here."

"What happens when the sun sets? Then how will we know?" asked Gabby.

"Oh, now that it's summer it won't set for a long time," Sydney assured her.

"Look at you, Ms. Nature! One year in the country, and you're navigating by the sun! *And* you know its whole schedule." Gabby felt something soft and sticky brush against her face, and then cling to it. She stopped walking. "*Ick!* Gross! What just got on me?" she said, plucking frantically at her shirt. "It's all over me!"

"It's just a spiderweb," Sydney told her. "You must have walked into it. Hold still and I'll get it off." She plucked the sticky strands off Gabby's face. "Did any get into your mouth?"

"Believe me, you'd know if it had gotten into my mouth," said Gabby. "I didn't know there were going to be *spiders* in this field."

Sydney laughed. "Did you think they only lived in apartments? Whether you're inside or outside, you're never farther than seven feet away from a spider. Truth! Anyway, we're almost there."

Now Gabby realized that the greenish light surrounding them was paler up ahead. "The two adventurers are about to escape from the jungle," she said. "And all because of Captain Costa's skills with the compass."

"*And* her medical skills after you were bitten by a bloodthirsty poisonous spider," Sydney reminded her.

They stepped out from behind the final row of corn—and stood still.

A huge parking lot, cracked and crumbled, lay before them. Behind it was the fairground. And the grown-ups had been right. This really *was* just an old abandoned plot of land. With old abandoned rides sprouting from it like a bunch of old toadstools. And faded NO TRESPASSING signs tacked to the rides and empty food stalls.

"I don't understand," Gabby said slowly. She stared at the old Ferris wheel. Its cars were swaying slightly, as if a wind were blowing them.

But it must have been a long, long time since anyone had taken a ride on that Ferris wheel.

"Looks like there's nothing much to see," said Sydney. "Do you want to head home?"

"*What?* And not investigate now that we're here?" exclaimed Gabby.

"But all those 'No Trespassing' signs . . ."

"Syd, come on. No one will see us. *No one.* Look how old those signs are. It's not as if this place is under surveillance!"

Gabby began walking briskly across the empty lot without even looking back to see if Sydney was following. Which, of course, she was.

When they'd crossed the parking lot, the girls realized that a sort of grass moat, like a long ditch, separated them from the fairground. "Do we have to wade through this?" asked Sydney.

"No, no. Look, there's a footpath." Gabby pointed to the far corner of the parking lot, and they headed toward the path. It led them to the fair's entrance: two peeling golden columns holding up a huge sign.

WELCOME TO THE TROUBLE SLOP AMUSEMENT PARK, it said.

"That's not a good sign, ha-ha," said Sydney. "I can't believe no one caught the missing *e*."

"Maybe the *e* fell off. But speaking of signs—there's that fun house I told you about. The one I saw from Aunt Lisa's car. It sure looks different, though."

The creepy painting of the magician had almost chipped away. His eyes—bright and menacing the night before—were just dark blurs now. The sign above the magician's open mouth was hanging by one corner, and it was so faded that Gabby had to squint to make out the words: THE MAGIC FUN HOUSE OF CLAUDIUS THE MAGNIFICENT. Every one of the colored lightbulbs that had been set around its border was either missing or smashed.

Sydney was staring at the sign with a strange expression on her face. "Gabby, didn't you tell me last night what that sign said?"

"Yes. I told you everything that happened."

"But—" Sydney stopped. "You couldn't have seen *this* sign from the road. Or at least you couldn't have read it.

But this is exactly what you told me it said!"

"You're right." Gabby took a deep breath. "And that means I was right too. It was lit up before! But . . . how? Sydney, do you realize that we're having an actual adventure?"

"I sure do," replied Sydney. "Let's go check everything out."

Together the two girls raced through the entrance.

Even though it was summer, everything about the fairground seemed to signal autumn. Part of that was because there were so many dead leaves everywhere. Falling leaves had filled entire seats on some of the rides. The horses on the merry-go-round were prancing over a floor of leaves, and clumps of leaves had blown into the games on the midway.

Something else was strange about the midway games. "Wouldn't you expect the owner to take this stuff with him?" Sydney asked, pointing at a moldy row of stuffed animals that had been used as prizes. What had once been a giant pink teddy bear lay on its back in a puddle next to a blue-polka-dotted giraffe that was missing one button eye. "They're not great prizes, but he could have given them to a hospital or something."

The ticket booth, too, seemed to have been abandoned while it was still in operation. Huge rolls of tickets were stacked inside, and an old hand stamper was still lying on the window ledge. And the cash register— "Hey, it's open!" said Gabby. But there was no money inside.

"Probably just as well," said Sydney. "It still would've been stealing if we'd taken it. Do you think it would be okay to take a roll of tickets, though? They might come in handy."

"Sure, no one will know," Gabby answered. But when Sydney picked up a roll, she put it down quickly. "Too soggy," she said with a shudder.

"I wonder if there's anything here that we could actually ride on, or play, or whatever," said Gabby. "Maybe up in that arcade? The door's open. Which is also weird," she added. "Even if you were closing down a fair, wouldn't you want to sell the stuff you *could* sell? I bet there are people out there who collect old arcade games."

Once they were inside the dark, gloomy arcade, Gabby changed her mind. "No one in the world would ever want this stuff," she said. "These games are so lame! Look at this one—Patty Cakes, it's called. I think all you have to do is hit the lights when they come on."

"They still play that kind of thing at fairs," returned Sydney. "Haven't you ever played Whac-A-Mole? But look at this video game—the Electric Eel." She gestured toward a console about the size of a drinking fountain. "The graphics are so lame. When was this invented? In the caveman days?"

Gabby knew that Sydney wasn't actually expecting an answer. But she'd been wondering the same thing herself. When was the last time this fair had been open to the public?

"Let's look around and see if there's any sign of a date on a poster or calendar or something," she suggested.

But the flyers that had been tacked up everywhere were too faded to read. And the girls couldn't find a calendar anywhere. Not even at the ticket booth, where it might have made sense to have one.

"Maybe we can find an old magazine or—or a concert program," Gabby suggested. "Sometimes there are concerts at fairs, right? Anyway, there's so much litter everywhere that we should be able to find something."

"Yes," agreed Sydney dubiously, "if we feel like rooting through litter. Which I don't. I think we should look around the entrance. People always post notices at the entrances to things."

"I don't see a single piece of paper anywhere," said Gabby when they'd returned to the entrance. "Do you?"

"Yup." Sydney said. She pointed. "Right over there on that gate."

Gabby blinked, astonished. She had just looked in that direction—and she was sure the bright neon-yellow sign hadn't been there a moment ago. There was no way she could have missed it! But Sydney was already running over to see what it said.

"Look, Gabs! It's for something called Kids' Week. Anyone under thirteen gets in free!"

"Is there a date on it?" asked Gabby.

Sydney didn't answer. She was staring at the notice.

"Syd?"

"There's a date," Sydney finally said. "But it's *this week*."

"What?" Gabby raced to Sydney's side.

Sydney was right. Kids' Week had started five days earlier, and it was still going on for two more nights.

The fair was supposed to open that very night, in . . . Gabby and Sydney both rummaged for their phones at the same time, but Gabby got there first.

"It's six," she said. "That means the fair opens in two hours."

Sydney gasped. "And supper at my house starts at six thirty! We'd better get going."

"Definitely," Gabby agreed. "If we eat fast, we can be here when it opens."

"When what opens?"

"The fair!" said Gabby. "What else have we been talking about?"

"But—" Sydney made a helpless gesture around them. "Look! How can anything be happening *here*? In all this mess?"

"I don't know, but something's going to happen. Maybe they just have a big party for kids, even though the rides don't work and you can't play the games. I don't know. But we've got to be here for it. We've *got* to!"

"I guess you're right," said Sydney slowly. "Although it sounds like kind of a lame party. But I'll ask Mom and Dad. If they say it's okay, then we can come."

Gabby's heart sank. Sydney's parents would never

agree to let the girls come here alone—not even if the girls managed to convince them that a run-down abandoned fair was really going to open that night. Back in San Francisco, the Costas had always walked Sydney over to Gabby's apartment building if it was dark out, even though the girls lived only a block apart.

I'll think about that later, she decided. Right now, what was important was getting back to Sydney's house on time.

The girls started toward the parking lot at a brisk walk that turned into a trot and then into full-fledged running. As they jogged along, Gabby noticed attractions she'd missed before. An Alpine Slide . . . swings . . . bumper cars . . .

Unfortunately, she didn't notice the rock in the path until she'd tripped over it at full speed. She pitched sideways and crashed into a small wooden kiddie theater to her right. Trying to steady herself, she grabbed the ragged curtain over the stage.

The curtain ripped off in her hands.

And out from behind it, a massive cloud of bats headed straight for the two girls.

CHAPTER 5

"VAMPIRES! *VAMPIRES!*"

Gabby was screaming without even realizing it. She threw herself to the ground, frantically covering her head with her hands. "My hair!" she shrieked. "They're biting me on the head! I'm bleeding!"

"Gabby. Gabby. Calm down." Sydney's voice was steady and quiet. "Nothing's happening. The bats flew away."

Cautiously, Gabby raised her head and peered up through her fingers. Sydney was right—there was no sign of a bat anywhere.

"Why did they leave?" she asked nervously.

Sydney laughed. "Probably because of all the yelling."

"Is—is it safe to stand up?"

"It was safe to stand up before! Wow, Gabs. You really do *not* like nature, do you?"

Slowly and a little self-consciously, Gabby got up. She patted her head with a tentative hand.

"No blood," she said, confused. "But I felt them biting me!"

Sydney looked as if she was trying not to laugh again. "Nothing was biting you. They weren't vampire bats."

"Well, then, why did they surround us like that?" demanded Gabby.

"They didn't surround us. They were sleeping in there! Bat colonies usually sleep in dark places during the day and go out to find food at night. These guys just left a little earlier than usual, is all."

"I hate nature," Gabby muttered. "There aren't any bats in San Francisco."

"Actually, there are," Sydney corrected her. "People just don't see them as often. And anyway, if it weren't for bats, there would be *way* more mosquitoes. It's weird, Gabby—you're so brave about things that could get us in trouble, but then you're scared of things like bats and spiders."

"When did you turn into Mother Nature?" Gabby snapped. She was a little hurt that Sydney thought she couldn't handle country life. Sydney never used to know anything about bats, of all things!

Now Sydney looked hurt. "I've always liked animals. You know that!"

"I knew you liked dogs and cats. I didn't know you liked *vermin*."

"I like all animals," Sydney snapped back. "And don't say 'vermin.' No animal is vermin." She sighed. "Let's just get back home."

This is awful, Gabby thought as the girls trudged along in silence. *We can't have a fight right at the beginning of my visit*. What would they do for the rest of the time if they weren't talking to each other? Gabby was almost starting to wish she hadn't come.

Sydney must have been thinking along the same lines. She cleared her throat and said, "My mom made lasagna because she knows it's your favorite."

"Yay! I love your mom's lasagna. Is she making garlic bread?"

Sydney grinned. "Do you even have to ask?"

Maybe we're just in bad moods because we're hungry and tired,

Gabby reflected. It was the kind of thing her parents always said—the kind of thing she hated to hear. "You're just hungry . . . You're just overexcited . . . Sounds like *someone's* ready for bed!" But now that she thought about it, Gabby realized that she was starving. And they *had* done a lot of walking that day.

Yes, things would be fine once she and Sydney had gotten something to eat. And then . . . the fair! If Sydney's parents would let them go . . .

To Gabby's surprise, they did. But it took some work on the girls' part.

"I wish we'd heard about this earlier so I could have checked it out," said Sydney's father.

"But Dad, I only just got the e-mail right before supper," said Sydney. (She and Gabby had agreed that telling Sydney's parents where the girls had *really* learned about Kids' Week was definitely a bad idea.)

"Are other kids you know going?" asked Mrs. Costa.

"Definitely," said Sydney. And it wasn't really a lie. She did know Gabby, after all.

Sydney's parents looked at each other for a second.

Then Mrs. Costa said, "I guess it's okay for you to walk over and check it out. But you'll need to be home by ten at the latest."

"Yay! Thanks, Mom and Dad!"

"Thanks, Mr. and Mrs. Costa!" Gabby echoed.

"Just be careful," warned Mr. Costa. "And bring flashlights with you. There are a couple hanging in the garage."

"Dad! We don't need actual flashlights," Sydney scolded. "We have flashlight apps on our phones."

"They'll use up the battery in two seconds," said Mr. Costa. "Humor me. Take the flashlights."

Sydney gave an exaggerated sigh. "Okay, okay. But really, thanks for letting us go. We'll be very careful."

"We'll win a prize and bring it home for you," Gabby added.

"Excellent," Sydney's mom said. "Just make sure it's not anything alive."

"I'm starting to feel as though we *live* in this cornfield," Gabby said. "Shouldn't we leave a trail of cookie crumbs to show where we've been?"

It was a little later, seven thirty. Once they'd gotten permission to go out, the girls had eaten as fast as they could. (Which didn't prevent Gabby from scarfing down a third helping of lasagna.) Now they were back in the same jungle of cornstalks, on their way to the fair. It was still light out, but a sliver of moon was just beginning to rise.

"I can't believe your parents let you walk around alone like this," said Gabby. "They were always so *supervise-y* of you in San Francisco."

"That's one great thing about living in the country," Sydney replied. "As long as I have my phone, I'm allowed to walk anywhere at pretty much any time."

"Lucky you," said Gabby. Secretly she was thinking that it wasn't much of a privilege to be walking through this dark cornfield. The sky above them was slow to lose its brightness, but surrounded by cornstalks, it felt much more shadowy. She was glad they had flashlights, but the thing about a flashlight was that it made every place you weren't aiming it seem even darker.

Gabby had already gotten six mosquito bites, and those were just the ones she knew about. She wasn't going to complain about them, though. She had complained enough about the great outdoors for one day.

Besides, she didn't want to fight with Sydney anymore.

"Look!" Sydney stopped so suddenly that Gabby almost bumped into her. "I can see lights. The fairground really is open! You were right!"

Compared with the dingy reality of what the girls had seen only a few hours before, the cluster of lights in the distance seemed almost like a mirage. How had people managed to light up the whole place so quickly?

"Kids' Week must be a big deal," Gabby said. Then she paused, thinking. She'd already seen the fair lit up like this just the night before. If it had been open then, why had the fair been such a wreck today? But the announcement the girls had found was definitely dated for this week.

Oh, well. Whatever was going on, Gabby still couldn't wait to get to the fair. "Let's race there," she suggested. She knew Sydney loved to run as much as she did. "We can use the rows of corn as lanes."

"Cool! What's the finish line?"

"The fair, duh!"

"No, that's not specific enough," Sydney objected. "Let's say the winner is the first person to reach the edge of the cornfield."

"Fine," said Gabby. Then she pushed her way through the thick stalks of corn to the next row.

"Okay, I'm in my lane," she reported. "Are you ready?"

"Bring it on," said Sydney.

"Okay. On your mark."

Gabby bent her knees and leaned forward.

"Get set."

She aimed her flashlight into the darkness ahead.

"Go!"

The two girls shot forward.

Gabby knew it was a waste of time to look around during a race, but after a couple of moments she was pretty sure that she was ahead of Sydney. The thing she had to watch out for was the bumpy, uneven dirt. If her foot touched the ground in the wrong way, she might end up twisting her ankle. *Slow and steady*, she cautioned herself.

But wait. Didn't *fast* and steady make more sense? Gabby trained her flashlight directly on the ground ahead of her. She would concentrate on the uneven dirt and stop worrying about what was in front of her.

She hadn't noticed before how hot and humid it was. Keeping a steady pace was getting harder now. Gabby could hear Sydney breathing hard behind her. "How are you doing back there?" she called.

"Just—just getting ready to pass you," Sydney panted back.

"Never! *Never!*"

Gabby steadied her own breath and reminded herself to pump her arms. A few more yards, and she was pretty sure she was pulling even farther ahead of Sydney. A few yards after that, and she couldn't hear her friend at all.

How much farther to go? Gabby raised her eyes toward the fair for a split second and realized that she had covered a lot of ground. The lights of the fair were much closer now. But where was Sydney? She was a good runner too. She shouldn't have fallen so far behind. . . .

Gabby half turned her head to call back over her shoulder. "Get up here, lazybones!"

And that instant when she looked away from the path was the instant that she tripped for the second time that day. Gabby had a split second to realize she was falling before she hit the ground so hard that it knocked the wind out of her. Her flashlight flew out of her hand. She heard it land with a little thud—but she couldn't see where it had fallen. The light had gone out.

Gabby's knee was throbbing from its collision with the ground, and she was gasping for air. When she'd gotten her breath back, she yelled back to Sydney.

"Syd, where are you? I fell!"

"Sydney?" she called again.

She couldn't hear anything. Not the pounding of Sydney's feet, not a rustle from the corn—nothing.

She was all alone in total darkness.

Don't panic. It wasn't total darkness, after all. Outside the cornfield, it was still twilight. It was only dark amid the stalks of corn.

Yes, but I'm deep in the cornfield. . . .

As quietly as she could, and agonizingly slowly, Gabby rose to her feet. She paused halfway to listen again.

Was that a breeze rustling the corn?

"S-Sydney? Is that you?"

Gabby's voice came out in a scared little croak. No one answered her.

Now she was sure that it hadn't been a breeze. Someone was brushing against the corn. Whoever—whatever—it was, the sound was coming closer.

Gabby wondered wildly if some kind of animal was creeping toward her. Should she make a noise to show it she wasn't afraid? Or would it be smarter to stay still? But she'd heard that animals could sense fear. . . .

Gabby's teeth were chattering. She pressed her lips together. Even such a small sound might give her away.

Suddenly she remembered her cell phone. She could call 911. But even if there was service out here, what should she say? After all, she had no idea where she was. "I'm trapped in a cornfield" wouldn't bring her any help. And she didn't want whatever was out there to hear her voice.

Still, the phone was the closest thing she had to a lifeline. Gabby was dying to yank it out of her pocket, but she knew she shouldn't draw attention to herself if she could help it. Her hand was shaking as she began to edge it out with her thumb and forefinger. She almost had it now. . . .

A hand shot out of the darkness behind her and gripped her arm.

CHAPTER 6

"Don't be scared," came Sydney's panting voice. "It's me."

She pulled back the cornstalks to peer at Gabby, then stepped through them.

Gabby had opened her mouth to scream. Instead she drew a huge, shaky breath. *"Sydney,"* she panted. "You almost scared me to death. *Literally.* Why didn't you tell me you were there?"

"I was trying to get my breath back!" said Sydney. "You were really sprinting for a while there. I was way behind when I heard you call me. I couldn't run and yell at the same time."

She bent over and rested her hands on her knees. "I'm *exhausted.*"

"Me too," said Gabby. "Let's rest for a minute before we start running again."

"Again? I'm done with the race," said Sydney. "I declare you the winner. Let's find your flashlight and just walk the rest of the way there." She switched on her own flashlight.

It didn't take long for them to find Gabby's light, which hadn't broken after all. Gabby brushed the dirt off it. "Good as new," she said.

Suddenly she paused, listening. "Do you hear that?"

A distant kaleidoscope of tunes from different rides. The steady, muffled hum of a generator. And, somehow, the sound of excitement.

"The fair!" Both girls said it at the same time. Then—almost as if they'd been hypnotized—they headed in the direction of the sounds.

"This. Is. Amazing," said Gabby a few minutes later.

"I can't believe it," Sydney replied. "How did they get everything fixed up so fast?"

Before them was a big, bustling amusement park. And every inch of it was in full operation.

The entrance gates were wide open. Kids were

streaming in from all sides. The Ferris wheel, wreathed in lights, spun slowly in the background.

The transformation seemed so magical that for a full minute the girls stood still, taking everything in. Then Gabby gave herself a shake. "So what do you want to do first? I vote the roller coaster. Doesn't it look great?"

It was named the Greased Spiderweb. AND YOU ARE THE FLY! proclaimed the sign at the entrance. There was a list of rules:

WARNING!!!

THIS HIGH-SPEED ROLLER COASTER RIDE TO THE "TOP OF THE WEB" INCLUDES SHARP TURNS, SUDDEN DROPS, SUDDEN CHANGES IN DIRECTION, STEEP TILTING, SPINS, AND BLACKOUT TUNNELS.

YOU MUST BE IN GOOD HEALTH TO PARTICIPATE IN THIS ADVENTURE. WE ARE NOT RESPONSIBLE FOR SUDDEN DEATH DUE TO HEART FAILURE.

NO RIDERS UNDER 48 INCHES IN HEIGHT. NO SENSITIVITY TO STROBE LIGHTS.

NO ARM OR LEG CASTS.

EXPECTANT MOTHERS SHOULD NOT RIDE.

PEOPLE WITH A FEAR OF HEIGHTS WOULD
BE INSANE TO RIDE.

ENJOY YOUR RIDE (IF YOU SURVIVE)!!!

"I vote to stay on the ground and watch you on the roller coaster," Sydney said firmly. "I haven't been on a roller coaster since I was at a birthday party a few years ago. I threw up on some man's head."

"You really don't mind if I go without you?"

"I *want* you to go without me. Really! When you're done, we'll find a ride we can do together. The Toddler Train over there looks about my speed."

The line for the roller coaster was just starting to move, so Gabby ran over. "Do I need tickets for this?" she asked the dark-haired attendant at the entrance.

He grinned at her. "Of course not! Everything's free for kids tonight. Didn't you know that?"

"I knew there was free admission, but—"

"Free admission and free rides!" said the attendant

cheerfully. "Hop aboard and we'll get started. Is anyone with you?"

"I'm on my own. The friend I came with is a coward," Gabby told him. "Do I have to ride in a car with someone I don't know?"

The attendant glanced quickly at the row of cars. "Nah, I don't think so. There aren't that many riders. Just get in and make yourself comfortable."

Gabby thanked him as she hopped into the next car. She never had as much fun on rides if she had to sit with strangers.

The Greased Spiderweb looked old-fashioned. The rails were made of wood that creaked at every turn. But the first time the cars dropped—which was about a second after the coaster had started moving—Gabby realized that this was going to be the most intense ride she'd ever taken. Up until now, she'd been sure there wasn't a ride out there that could scare her. She'd *never* had a fear of heights. She'd *never* been uncomfortable if she was upside down. She'd *always* raised her arms in the air at scary moments instead of clutching the safety bar. On the Greased Spiderweb, it was all she could do to keep her hands from covering her face.

"BEST EVER!" yelled a guy close behind her. "Woo-hoooooooooooooooo!"

How could he be having fun? Suddenly Gabby wished she'd been seated next to someone. Even a total stranger. What if her seat belt broke and she slid over and there was no one to grab her and—

Stop. Don't think about it, she told herself quickly.

When the cars went into a blackout tunnel and then flipped over, Gabby gave up and scrunched down in her seat with her eyes closed. Her legs were shaking when the ride ended and she walked dizzily over to Sydney.

"Ready to go again?" joked Sydney.

"Uhhhhhh. Don't even think about it. I'm not sure I'll ever *walk* again. Can we sit down on that bench over there? By the snack bar?"

Without waiting for an answer, Gabby walked over to the bench, plunked herself down, and buried her face in her hands. Sydney sat down next to her. "Are you going to throw up?" she asked sympathetically.

"No, I'm just dizzy." Gabby sat up and pushed her hair back. "I can't believe they fixed up that roller coaster so fast! Didn't it look as though it had fallen apart this afternoon?"

"I didn't notice. I don't even like to look at roller coasters when they're sitting still. But all the rides here look incredible compared to this afternoon. And they all work! I could've sworn some of the stuff was too smashed up ever to be used again."

"Very weird," said Gabby. "Maybe it's getting too dark for us to see all the rust."

"I was going to say that maybe the lights are making everything look new. But whatever. Do you feel okay now? Want to find another ride?"

Two girls who were a little older than Gabby and Sydney passed by. They were arguing loudly.

"It's not a *fair* without cotton candy," one of them was saying. "I don't want to leave until we get some."

Her friend sighed. "We've already had popcorn and deep-fried candy bars and those stupid oversize lollipops. Can't we just imagine we've had cotton candy, too?"

"No way," the first girl said firmly. "We're going to track down some cotton candy even if it takes us all night."

When the two girls had passed, Gabby turned to Sydney. "For some reason, I suddenly got this craving for cotton candy. Do you want any?"

Sydney thought it over. "Not yet. But I'll come with

you. Where did those girls say the cotton candy stand was?"

"I didn't see where they headed. But it's got to be nearby."

The strange thing was that they couldn't see a cotton candy stand anywhere. There were stands selling corn dogs and popcorn and funnel cakes, but where was the cotton candy?

"Let's ask over at that snack bar," Gabby finally said. But when they got there, no one was at the counter.

"They must be taking a break," said Sydney. "It's weird, though—have you noticed that there's hardly anyone working here? Look over there. The ice-cream booth is empty, and so is the pretzel stand. We're not just supposed to walk in and take food, are we?"

"You can't take cotton candy, anyway. You have to make it in that—"

A man's sudden shout made both girls jump.

"COT-ton candy!" the man was yelling. "Get your fresh cotton candy!"

He was standing next to a wheeled cotton-candy cart about ten feet away from the girls. Gabby couldn't believe they had just walked right by the cart.

"Wow! Um, g-great," she stammered. "I'd like some."

"Comin' right up!" said the cotton-candy man cheerfully.

Gabby stared at him. "Wait—didn't I just see you at the roller coaster?"

"I wear a lot of hats at this fair," the man said. "That's how it goes when you're a carny."

"What's a carny?" asked Gabby.

"A carny's someone who works at a carnival! Although this isn't really a carnival. Fairs stay put; carnivals travel. But I have so many jobs around here that I guess calling me a carny is pretty close to the truth."

He was swirling the clouds of pink sugar as he chatted. "Nice crowd tonight. That's great for us. We can sure use the business. Okay . . . almost done . . . and there we go!" With a flourish, he held up a billowy pink mountain of cotton candy on top of a paper cone.

As Gabby rummaged around for her money, she turned aside to whisper to Sydney. "I should have asked if he had the blue raspberry kind. It's my favorite."

Wallet in hand, she turned back to the cotton-candy man. "I forgot to ask how much it—"

The fluff of candy on the cone he was holding was now bright blue.

CHAPTER 7

Gabby stared at the cotton candy. Blue. Definitely blue. She held out her wallet in silence because she couldn't think of a thing to say.

The carny shook his head vigorously. "Oh, there's no charge. This is Kids' Week, remember? Free admission, free rides, free food."

Gabby finally found her voice. "Is *everything* here free?"

"You bet. Put that wallet away. And have a great night now!" Whistling, he began to wheel the cart away.

The two girls stared at each other.

"Did—did that just happen?" asked Gabby.

"The color, you mean? Yes. Definitely. It started out pink and changed to blue."

"Does cotton candy *do* that?"

Sydney sounded doubtful. "If it does, I've never heard of it. Gabby, are we going crazy?"

"We can't both be going crazy if we're seeing the same things," said Gabby. She looked suspiciously down at the cotton candy. "I hope this *is* cotton candy."

"Better not try it," advised Sydney. "Anything that can change color that fast can't be real food."

Gabby sniffed the blue puff of candy. "Smells okay." She pulled off a tiny wisp and spun it between her fingers. "It feels normal. I'm going to trust it."

"No, don't!"

But Gabby was already taking a big bite. "Mmm. Blue raspberry. Want some?"

"No way," said Sydney. "And if I were you, I wouldn't— Wait! Watch out!"

A boy about their age was walking backward to talk to his friends. He was so involved in whatever he was saying that he didn't seem to notice that he was about to collide with Gabby until he'd stepped on her foot. When he tried to get out of her way, he tripped—and took Gabby down with him as he stumbled.

"What's your problem?" yelled Gabby at the same time that the boy began to apologize.

"I'm really sorry," he said, scrambling to his feet. He looked anxiously down at her. "Are you okay?"

Wincing, Gabby stood up and took a couple of hobbling steps. She looked sadly at her cotton candy, which had flown out of her hands and lay covered in dirt a few yards away. "I guess so," she said.

"Are you sure?" the boy asked. His friends were standing behind him in a little cluster, silently waiting to see what would happen.

"Really. I'm fine." For the first time Gabby realized how good-looking the boy was. He had dark-brown hair and very blue eyes. And he did look sorry for having crashed into her.

"I'm fine," she repeated. Right away, she wanted to kick herself. Why had she said it twice?

"Well—uh—okay, then. That's good. Sorry again! See you around."

He gave her an awkward wave and walked quickly away as his friends hurried to catch up with him.

"He's cute," Sydney said. "That whole thing was

cute—how he tripped you and then apologized. Did you see that he was blushing?"

"Shut up. He was not."

"He was! I wonder who he is," mused Sydney. "He doesn't go to my school."

"It doesn't matter who he is," Gabby pointed out, "since we're never going to see him again." *Too bad,* she found herself thinking. She hurried to change the subject. "Let's go to the fun house, okay? We've got to get some more use out of this fair."

The fun house was a long, low building painted black with garish neon trim. The paint was fresh and shiny. The sign over the doorway also looked freshly painted. Gleaming black-and-silver streamers hung from the doorway itself—or the magician's open mouth, depending on how you wanted to think of it. From inside the fun house, the girls could hear horror-movie music punctuated by recorded screams and diabolical laughter. There was no one in line. In fact, the fun house seemed to be deserted. But Gabby didn't care.

"What are we waiting for?" she said. "Let's go in!"

Sydney stood still for a second, gazing up at the magician's face. "Does he look familiar to you?"

Gabby laughed. "I don't know a lot of evil magicians."

"No, really. Doesn't he look a little bit like the cotton candy guy—the carny, he called himself? He has the same eyebrows."

When she actually looked at the painting, Gabby could see what Sydney meant. "Maybe they're related," she said. "Maybe a family owns this fair. Maybe it's just a coincidence. Does it matter? Let's go in."

A superbright strobe was flashing just inside the doorway. It lit the way to another doorway. Once the girls had stepped through that, they stopped abruptly: Past the second doorway, there was no more light at all. They were standing in a pitch-black space, waiting to see what would happen next.

"STEP FORWARD IF YOU DARE," a deep voice commanded them. A flurry of high, shrill voices took up the command from all over the ceiling. *"Step forward step forward step forward step forward!"*

The girls took a couple of uncertain steps, and a red spotlight suddenly beamed onto the figure of a purple-gowned man sitting stiffly in a high, carved chair. He was wearing a striped turban with a green glass jewel in the center. His painted eyes slid back and forth, and every few seconds they blinked with a clanking sound.

"MEET ZANTINAR," said the deep voice. As if on cue, the man's plaster arm snapped forward. In his painted hand was a ticket. When Gabby took it, the arm snapped down again. "Press Button for Fortunes" was printed on the ticket. Now she noticed the brass button on the arm of the man's chair.

"Sydney, you go first," she said.

When Sydney pressed the button, a whirring sound came from somewhere inside the man. His eyes blinked rapidly as a cloud of smoke rose from his turban. Then his arm snapped forward again. This time he was holding a fortune printed on a slip of paper.

"'Prepare for a departure,'" Sydney read aloud. "That's dumb. It could mean anything. In a few minutes, we'll be departing this building."

"Fortunes have to be kind of general," Gabby pointed out. "Otherwise they wouldn't work for enough people. I'll try now."

It seemed to take longer for Gabby's fortune to appear—but when Zantinar finally held out his hand, the fortune Gabby picked up was even shorter than Sydney's had been.

LEAVE. NOW.

She showed the fortune to Sydney and then stuffed it into her pocket. "Totally lame. Leave the fun house? Leave the fair? Leave this room? Whoever is writing these should get a new job. Let's keep going."

The next room was the Vortex Chamber, where the girls had to crawl across a spinning floor while being blasted by whirlwind air jets from the ceiling. Next came the Tilting Room, which became extra-exciting when Sydney's wallet fell out of her pocket and slid away. (They found it in a corner.) The girls were patted on the head by gooey phosphorescent Goblin Fingers, buried up to their ankles in the Desert of Quicksand, and annoyed in the Maze of Tombstones, where every dead end held some kind of haunted-house special effect. "If we end up looking at the Headless Woman one more time, I'm going to scream out of *boredom*," Gabby announced.

It took three more Headless Woman dead ends, plus being trapped twice by the Ghoulish Guillotine, before Gabby and Sydney finally escaped the maze. Now they had reached the last room in the fun house—the Hall of Mirrors.

This room was decorated to look medieval. Crossed swords hung on the walls. Fake stone gargoyles peeked out of the corners. The mirrors were set into ornately carved frames that made each reflection look like a mildewed old portrait. The reflections in the mirrors certainly weren't the ordinary squished-down or super-widened distortions. These mirrors turned the girls into images of zombies, monsters, and witches. One showed them how they would look in coffins; another made it look as if they were walking through flames.

The only sound effect was a moaning wind. The room was lit by rows of candles—fake, but very realistic. Their flickering light made each reflection even creepier.

"Okay. This room, I give an A plus," Gabby declared. "What's that mirror over there?"

It was the biggest one in the room, so the girls were expecting it to have the biggest special effects. They were surprised when their own ordinary reflections looked back at them.

"Are we supposed to do something to get it started?" asked Sydney.

"Maybe." Gabby waved her arms. Her reflection waved its arms back. She stuck out her tongue, and her reflection stuck its tongue out. She reached out and took Sydney's hand . . .

. . . and her reflection didn't budge.

"How do they do that?" whispered Sydney. She let go of Gabby's hand. But in the mirror, both girls stood still.

Then the flickering candles went out one by one until the room was completely black.

"You're still there, right?" asked Sydney.

"Yes. Here's my hand—my real hand." Hand in hand, the girls stood motionless and wondered what to do. The sound of the recorded wind swirled around them.

"I guess we'll have to find the exit in the dark," Gabby said. "There has to be an exit sign, right? I think it's the law."

Before Sydney could answer, a single candle flickered back on, then another.

In the mirror, the girls' reflections relaxed—

—and then showed two faces that were petrified with shock.

There was a third reflection in the mirror.

CHAPTER 8

In the dim light the girls watched, frozen, as the reflected figure stepped toward their own reflections. And for the second time that evening, someone said, "Don't be scared." Both girls turned around, but Gabby already knew who it was. As soon as he'd spoken, she had recognized the cute boy who'd bumped into her earlier.

He looked sheepish now. "I've got to figure out how to meet people more easily," he said. "Bumping into them and scaring them to death make for bad impressions."

Gabby giggled, relieved. "You think? Maybe it would be easier just to tell us your name."

"Good idea. I'm Tyler Fields. And who are you guys?"

"I'm Gabby Carter. And this person next to me who

looks as if she's going to faint is my best friend, Sydney Costa."

"I'm not going to faint," Sydney said indignantly. "I was surprised, that's all. I'm not used to having people sneak up on me."

"I didn't mean to startle you guys, I swear. I just noticed that—well—I had never seen you at this fair before, and I wanted to meet you." He grinned. "Also, I never miss a chance to go through the fun house. It's cool, isn't it?"

"Definitely," said Gabby. "Kind of old-fashioned, but that's one thing I like about it."

"So this is your first time here?"

"Yes—and my first time in Iowa. I'm visiting Sydney. We only found out about the fair this afternoon."

"That's too bad," Tyler said, "because after tomorrow night it closes until next year. Well, I guess you'd better make the most of it. Do you guys want to go on a ride or something?"

"Sure!" said Gabby. "What do you recommend?"

"This might sound lame," said Tyler, "but why don't we go on the merry-go-round? We could sit in one of those booths they have."

"Booths on a *merry-go-round?*" exclaimed Gabby indignantly. "Those are where, like, moms sit so they'll be near their kids!"

Sydney chimed in, "Every kind of ride scares me, but even I would never sit in a booth."

"Yeah, I know, but they're the only ride-type thing where it's quiet enough to talk," Tyler pointed out. "Anyway, I don't see why people should outgrow merry-go-rounds. They're not scary, but they're fun."

Gabby liked him for saying that. It meant that he wasn't trying to show off. "All right. You've convinced me," she said. "Let's go."

As the three of them headed down the fun house exit ramp, Gabby became aware of a strange feeling—a kind of itch between her shoulder blades. She'd felt that itch before: It meant someone was staring at her. Was someone following them down the ramp? Gabby glanced over her shoulder, but there was no one there. She looked to either side, but none of the fairgoers was paying attention to her. Still, the feeling was getting stronger. Although Sydney and Tyler didn't seem to have noticed, Gabby was sure someone was watching them walk away.

Away. Why had that word come into her head? The

only thing they were walking away from was the fun house. Did that mean someone at the fun house was watching them?

Again Gabby looked over her shoulder. No one was looking at them except the painting of the evil magician around the fun house entrance, which was right next to the exit. And of course he wasn't really looking at them.

Except for the fact that at that moment, he winked at Gabby.

She stopped in her tracks and stared at the painting. Nothing moved. Why should it? The magician was only a painting—flat and harmless, his unseeing eyes staring out at nothing. And of course he hadn't really winked at Gabby. . . .

But she was sure he had.

I don't make stuff up, she told herself. *When I thought this fair was real, I turned out to be right. So if I saw the magician wink, he probably did wink.*

Come to think of it, though, she might have imagined that she thought someone was watching. There was no way of proving a feeling. What if she had seen the magician wink because she *expected* it? If, because she couldn't spot any live people looking at her, she had subconsciously "forced" the magician painting to confirm her suspicion?

When Sydney's voice broke into her thoughts, Gabby realized that the other two kids had been staring at her. "Gabs? What's the matter?"

"For a second I thought I'd left something at the fun house," Gabby lied. "But I couldn't have, could I?" She fell back into step with Sydney and Tyler. The feeling that someone was watching her had vanished, but it had been replaced by a much creepier idea.

Either the magician had winked, or Gabby's imagination was making her see things that weren't there.

I'm not going to think about it anymore. I'm going to pay attention to what's really happening right now.

Tyler had been right. It *was* easy to talk in the booth at the merry-go-round. He was a good listener, too. He asked both girls lots of questions about themselves, and he didn't talk about himself too much. In fact, he hardly talked about himself at all.

"You said you noticed we were new here," Gabby said at one point. "Does that mean you come here a lot?"

"I practically live here," Tyler confessed. "Or that's what it feels like sometimes."

"Well, *I've* lived in Trouble Slope for a whole year," said Sydney, "and I can't believe I never knew about this fair until tonight. Is it open all summer?"

For some reason, Tyler looked uncomfortable. "Not all summer, no. I think it's kind of a special-occasion thing."

"You mean for things like Kids' Week?" asked Sydney.

"Uh-huh," said Tyler.

Sydney pressed on. "It's crazy that no one knows about Kids' Week, though. I haven't seen anyone from my school here. Gabby and I were downtown this morning, and there were no flyers or posters or anything. If we hadn't been—uh—investigating this afternoon, we would never have found out that the fair was going to be open. It's not as though there's a lot to do here in the summertime. They need better publicity!"

"Yeah, I guess," Tyler said unenthusiastically.

"And if it's just open once in a while, they should have more people working here," Sydney added. "Look at that ice cream place over there. It's empty! Don't they want to sell stuff?"

There was a short, uncomfortable silence before

Tyler said, "It's Kids' Week. I guess they want us to help ourselves. I don't know."

Either he was bored, or he didn't like talking about this. So it was probably lucky that before the conversation could disintegrate any further, another boy their age strode up to the merry-go-round.

"Where've you been, Ty?" the boy called, loping alongside them. "Danielle says to—" Then he caught sight of Gabby and Sydney. "Oh. Sorry. Who are they?"

"This is Gabby, and this is Sydney," Tyler said. "It's their first time here." To Gabby and Sydney, he said, "This is my friend Austin."

"Hey," Austin said. Panted, really. Keeping pace with the merry-go-round was starting to take a toll on him. His face was red, and he was all sweaty.

Tyler must have noticed. "Stop chasing this thing, dude! Wait and get on with us for the next ride."

"How 'bout if I just get on now?" And before they knew what was happening, Austin had leaped up and grabbed the railing that encircled the platform of the merry-go-round.

He'd obviously meant to swing himself up, but he missed his footing. Instead of vaulting aboard, he ended up hanging on to the rail with both hands and dangling over the edge of the platform with his feet in the air.

"Whoa. This isn't good!" he gasped.

Tyler had jumped to his feet. "Just let go!"

"No, don't! Keep holding on! If he lets go, he'll fall underneath the platform and get pulverized!" wailed Sydney. Now she stood up too, reaching forward to grab Austin's wrists. "Help me, you guys!"

Tyler took Austin by the forearms, pulling as hard as he could. At the same time, Gabby was leaning over the railing and trying to get hold of Austin's shirt. For a second she thought she had him, but suddenly the shirt ripped out of her hands. Desperately, Gabby leaned out even farther and gripped two of the belt loops on his shorts. Then, with a mighty heave, she yanked him off the ground and into the booth.

Austin landed sprawling at their feet, a stunned look on his face.

"Are you okay?" the three of them asked at the same time.

"I don't know yet!" said Austin, annoyed. "Give me a chance to find out!"

"But *are* you okay?" Sydney persisted.

Austin seemed to be noticing her for the first time. His frown disappeared instantly. "Yeah, I think so." He got up and sat next to her, rubbing his wrists. "You're Sydney, right? You have a mighty grip."

Sydney smiled bashfully. "I'm glad you're okay."

"Me too!" said Austin cheerfully. "I would have hated to fall underneath the platform and get pulverized."

Now Sydney was blushing. "Okay, so I overreacted," she said. "But you really *would* have been hurt if you'd let go."

The merry-go-round was starting to slow down. "Let's go around one more time," Austin suggested. "Sitting next to Sydney will help me recover."

Wow, Gabby thought. Instant chemistry! She looked over at Tyler to see if he'd noticed. When he saw her, he rolled his eyes. "I think I'll go get something to drink," he said. "Want anything, Gabby?"

"Come to think of it, I'm thirsty too," Gabby answered. "You guys stay on if you want, though."

"I don't mind taking one more ride," Sydney said, a little too casually. "We'll catch up with you guys when it's over."

"That was quick," Tyler remarked as he and Gabby hopped off the merry-go-round.

"*Really* quick," Gabby agreed. "I didn't actually want something to drink—did you?"

"Nope. I just wanted to, you know, get out of their way. We should probably stop staring at them, though."

Gabby hadn't realized she was staring. She'd been studying Austin and wondering why both he and Tyler looked different from the kids she knew. It was something about their clothes, she decided. Like pretty much everyone their age, the boys were wearing T-shirts and jeans. But their jeans somehow had a different shape from what Gabby was used to. And their shoes were—well—just plain canvas high-tops. Not running shoes or basketball shoes, and not a brand Gabby had ever heard of.

The difference was nothing she could put her finger on. Maybe kids just dressed differently in this part of the country. . . .

"Do you guys live in Trouble Slope?" asked Gabby. She was thinking that Sydney's summer would be much more interesting if Austin was within easy reach.

Once again Tyler looked uncomfortable being asked what seemed, to Gabby, like a perfectly normal question. "Actually, we don't," he said.

"So . . . then . . . you come to the fair a lot because—?"

It was getting dark out, but Gabby was pretty sure Tyler's face had turned red. This was someone who did *not* like questions. Gabby decided to change the subject.

"I haven't seen Sydney for a year," she told Tyler. "We were best friends in San Francisco for our whole lives. Then her parents got jobs here. I think maybe she's changed a little since I last saw her."

"That wouldn't be too surprising after a year," said Tyler. "Anyway, it would be worse if she never changed at all. I mean, if she just stayed the same forever."

"Yeah, I guess so," Gabby agreed. "But if you see a friend all the time, maybe you don't notice the changes as much."

"You must have missed her a lot. But at least she's just one person to miss," Tyler observed.

"What do you mean?" asked Gabby.

Tyler shuffled his feet.

"I—uh—well, it would be harder if you missed lots of people, that's all. Sometimes that happens."

What could she say to *that*? Gabby wondered why her conversations with Tyler seemed to keep going in and out of focus. Maybe it was because even though he was perfectly nice, the two of them *hadn't* had instant chemistry like Sydney and Austin. He was cute, but that definitely wasn't everything. She saw with relief that the merry-go-round was stopping again. "We're over here!" she called to Sydney.

"Tyler, I just remembered something," said Austin as he and Sydney approached. "The thing I came over to say: Danielle wants you to come meet everyone by the Flying Scooters. They're probably waiting there now."

"Oh, man. She'll be in a bad mood about having waited so long," said Tyler. He turned to Gabby. "Want to meet some more of our friends?"

There turned out to be three of them—two girls and another boy. They were perched on a railing, chatting. As Tyler and Austin approached, one of the girls jumped off the railing and smiled.

"Where have you guys been?" she asked. But her smile immediately disappeared when she noticed Gabby and Sydney.

"We were riding the merry-go-round with some new friends," said Tyler. He gestured toward Gabby, who was standing a little behind him. "Everyone, meet Gabby. She's visiting for a week. And this is Sydney, who lives in Trouble Slope. They've never been here before," Tyler continued.

The other girl and boy who'd been perched on the railing jumped to their feet. "Hi! I'm Allie," said the girl. She had a round, sunburned face and a mop of curly red hair. She was wearing a T-shirt, denim cutoffs, and strappy sandals. Around her neck was a leather cord with a silver pendant in the shape of a peace sign.

"And I'm Will."

Will had sandy hair that reached his shoulders. He was wearing a shirt with a superhero logo and wide denim bell-bottoms. (Bell-bottoms! Gabby couldn't believe it. And the shirt was horrible too.) The first girl, who had to be Danielle, was wearing a flowy top and denim cutoffs. She had long, white-blond hair that was pulled into two pigtails, and she was deeply tanned. She would have been cute if she hadn't been wearing frosted blue eye shadow—and if she hadn't had such a sour look on her face.

She didn't introduce herself, so Tyler had to do it for her. "This is Danielle," he said. "So, Danielle . . . Austin said you wanted me to meet you all?"

"I thought we were going to go on some rides." Danielle sounded as if she was biting off the words. She looked at Tyler. "But maybe you have other plans?"

"Not really," said Tyler easily. "What do you guys think?" he asked Gabby and Sydney. Danielle continued to glare at them.

"Uh, whatever anyone wants to do is fine," Gabby sputtered.

"Let's definitely go on some rides!" said Sydney, beaming at Austin. She seemed oblivious to Danielle's wrath. "I *love* rides."

That was news to Gabby. All of a sudden, Sydney seemed to love the whole world.

"All right, then," said Danielle. She flicked her eyes toward Gabby. "Are you ready?"

Gabby nodded. She didn't quite trust her voice. Danielle had gotten so angry so quickly that she was still trying to process it.

Was Danielle jealous? Was she always this mean to outsiders? And even if the answer to both those questions was yes, why was she being so *extreme*?

Gabby had no idea. All she knew was that for the first time in her life, she'd met someone who genuinely seemed to hate her.

CHAPTER 9

I don't want to hear one more word out of Danielle, Gabby thought grimly as they trudged through the fair, debating which ride to go on. Hoping to head off any more nastiness, she asked, "What do you guys think is the best ride here?"

That did the trick. "The Space-a-Tron! Absolutely," said Tyler.

"The Space-a-Tron is far out," Will agreed.

"*And* it has real computers," added Allie. "Do you guys want to try it?"

What did Allie mean by "real" computers? Gabby couldn't wait to find out. But when they arrived at the Space-a-Tron, she and Sydney both burst out laughing.

The Space-a-Tron looked like a very old school bus that had been painted to look like a spaceship.

"Did they get this off eBay?" asked Sydney.

The question dropped into emptiness. All five kids were staring at Sydney and Gabby.

"You're *not* telling me you don't know what eBay is!" exclaimed Gabby.

"Ohhhhh, you said *eBay*," said Tyler quickly. "I didn't know you meant *that* eBay."

Austin spoke up almost as fast. "I didn't hear you at first. But yeah, I think they did get it for eBay."

For eBay? thought Gabby. Maybe Tyler and Austin didn't have the Internet where they lived. Gabby didn't want to embarrass them. It was probably better not to ask them any more questions.

Just then the bus bumped up awkwardly next to Gabby and her friends. "Next group!" called the attendant.

"Well, Gabby? Are you ready to go into outer space?" asked Tyler.

I didn't realize that outer space had been designed by pre-schoolers, Gabby thought.

The ride was on a conveyor-belt. As soon as everyone

had fastened their "space belts," the ship lurched forward. Then they progressed slowly along a winding path of lame space clichés while a recorded narrator described each new wonder.

"We have conquered the moon," announced the narrator. "Yet we still have no idea what beings inhabit that mysterious sphere . . . are they typical space creatures?" The ship was now passing a roomful of blob-like creatures wearing what seemed to be green shower curtains. They were making strange squeaks and popping noises.

"Or are they more humanoid?" the announcer continued. This room displayed four mannequins—two adults and two children—sitting around a plastic table. Apparently you were supposed to know they were aliens because they had antennae.

"More Venusian omelet, Rigel?" the mother humanoid asked.

Gabby was openmouthed. This was like a TV show from ancient history!

The spaceship bumped along to the next room, where blurry black-and-white footage of NASA engineers was being projected onto a wall. "To land the craft, these men will need *your* help," intoned the announcer. "Prepare to operate the computers!"

On cue, a door in the back of each seat slid open to reveal a thick, boxy keyboard attached to a postcard-size monitor with a gray screen.

"First, a few simple calculations are required."

"Simple" was right. On the screen appeared an arithmetic problem:

$$12 \times 2 =$$

"You have to use the keys here to make the answers appear on the screen," said Tyler. He pecked at the keyboard with one index finger.

"Splendid. Now we must chart a course for the vessel," continued the narrator. A small, dim cursor appeared on the screen.

"First, move the signalizer north."

"What's a signalizer?" asked Gabby.

"*That!*" Tyler pointed at the cursor. "You move it with the arrow keys—look. You can even make it go in a circle!"

"Um . . . okay. Can I have a turn?"

Tyler looked surprised. "Are you interested in

computers? They seem like more of a boy thing to me."

Gabby was starting to feel as if she herself was in outer space. *This* was the computer Tyler had been so excited about? And he thought computers were just for boys? Did these kids live in a cave somewhere?

I have to be polite. I can't make fun of this stuff. "I don't really need a turn. You go ahead."

The recording went droning on. "Splendid! Now we prepare to bring the ship in for a landing. . . ."

When the Space-a-Tron ride had finally ended, and they were heading out the back exit, Gabby hurried to catch up with Sydney. "Did you believe that ride?" she whispered.

But thanks to Austin, Sydney had entered her own personal outer space. She didn't seem to have heard Gabby's question.

"You know what I'd love to do now?" Sydney asked. "The beeper cars."

"Beeper cars?" said Allie.

"You know—where you drive around in a little toy car and beep your horn a lot. It's so much fun!"

"Do you mean the bumper cars?" asked Will after a second.

Sydney looked confused. "It's not 'beeper'? I know I've seen people in those little cars beeping at one another."

"You realize that's not the point of the ride, though, right?" said Will hesitantly.

"Of course not! You get to drive the little car, not just honk the horn!"

"Sydney, have you ever been in a bumper car?" That was Austin.

"Nope," said Sydney cheerfully. "But there's a first time for everything."

"Well, the point is not that you get to honk the little horn," said Danielle. "The point is that you ram your car into other people's cars. You 'bump' them. Get it?"

Now Sydney looked confused. "But why is that fun?"

I'd better help her out, Gabby thought. She tried to make her voice hearty and enthusiastic. "You'll see why as soon as you get into your car. I vote for the bumper cars too!"

Sydney was disappointed when they got into line and she found out that each bumper car only held one person. "I don't want to be alone if someone hits me!"

"Why don't you look at the people in the cars?" Danielle couldn't have sounded snottier. "See how

93

they're *laughing*? See how the cars have *rubber bumpers* so no one can get hurt? See how this is supposed to be *fun*?"

"Give it a rest, Danielle," snapped Austin. "She said she's never done this before."

Danielle shrugged. "Then I hope she's prepared for serious danger."

It was lucky that their group was at the front of the line. The gate opened, and they didn't have to talk anymore.

Gabby picked a car at the edge of the rink, but she didn't start driving right away. She was trying to figure out what was happening with Danielle.

There were only two explanations as to why Danielle was being so horrible, particularly to her. First, maybe she was always horrible. But it was hard to imagine the other four kids being friends with her if she acted like that all the time. Plus, she had been smiling when they had first approached. More likely, she was jealous—which was so stupid that it made Gabby mad. She had known Tyler for about forty-five minutes. How could she possibly be a threat to Danielle?

If Gabby had fallen for Tyler the instant she met him, Danielle might—*might*—have had a reason to be mad.

But Gabby had quickly realized that she didn't have even the tiniest crush on Tyler, even if she did think he was cute. And she hadn't picked up any hint that that Tyler was interested in being more than friends with her. Besides, Danielle knew that Gabby was going back home in a few days. She would have the rest of her life to win Tyler back if she needed to!

CRASH!

Someone rammed Gabby's bumper car from behind—*hard*. Startled, she turned to see who'd hit her, but it was impossible to tell. Every car on the rink had a driver, and every driver was happily bashing around. Across the room, she could see Sydney beaming as she honked the horn over and over, and even laughing as Will gently bumped his car into hers.

I'd better join in or people will notice me. One good thing: She wouldn't have to talk to Danielle while she was driving. . . .

But as Gabby wove in and out of the traffic, she started to wonder if something was the matter with her car. The hits she was taking were so hard, and so frequent. It was one thing to bang your car into a friend's and feel a little bounce. You weren't supposed to be crashed into so hard that you got whiplash!

Maybe she should try to get her car back to the edge of the rink. Of course, these cars didn't drive in a straight line, so—

CRASH!

Once again someone had rear-ended her car. This time, Gabby accidentally bit her lip so hard that she tasted blood. Furious, she whipped around to see who was behind her—and caught Danielle backing up to ram her car one more time. Strangely, Danielle didn't look angry. Instead she had a look of intense concentration, like someone on a mission.

But Gabby was angry. "Get *out* of here!" she shouted at Danielle. It wasn't the most useful thing to say, since there was no way either of them could go anywhere until the ride was over. But at least Danielle stayed away from Gabby for the rest of the time.

"Is something the matter?" murmured Tyler when they were back out on the pavement. "You look kind of upset."

"I'm going to be upset for the rest of my life," snapped Gabby. "Danielle is totally out to get me. What is her *problem?*"

Tyler sighed. "I wish I knew. She's kind of bossy, but I've never seen her like this."

"Are you going out with her?"

"No! I mean, I—I don't think so. We always hang around with the group. I'm not sure I've ever been alone with her."

"I could be wrong. But I'm guessing that Danielle has a different take on your relationship," Gabby said.

She was starting to think she'd had enough of Kids' Week.

Sydney, on the other hand, was glowing with happiness. Meeting Austin seemed almost to have turned her into a different person—outgoing, flirty, and more talkative than Gabby had ever seen her.

"I can't believe how great this fair is," she gushed. "And Austin says the Ferris wheel just opened. They were doing some repairs on it before. But he says it's more fun in the dark, anyway."

It was definitely dark now. Really dark. So dark that Gabby suddenly remembered their curfew.

"Syd, what time is it?" she asked. "It must be late!" She started to pull her phone out of her pocket, but Tyler had already checked his wristwatch.

"It's nine thirty-seven."

"We've got to get home," Gabby said nervously.

"Just one ride on the Ferris wheel first." Austin was smiling at Sydney as he spoke. "It will only take a few minutes."

"Well . . . okay," said Sydney. "I'm sure my parents won't mind if we're a little late."

Gabby stared at her, amazed. "*Your* parents? Your parents call the police if you get a hangnail! We *have* to go." Was she going to have to *drag* Sydney home?

"It's a good idea," Danielle put in. "Ten is pretty late for some kids."

No one paid any attention to her. At that moment, Austin and Sydney had center stage.

"Come back tomorrow night, then," he was coaxing Sydney. "It's the last night of Kids' Week. We *need* to go on the Ferris wheel together. I'm serious. Promise me you will!"

"I promise. Cross my heart and hope to die."

Behind Austin's back, Danielle rolled her eyes. Gabby could almost sympathize with her.

"We might have other plans," Gabby warned Sydney. "Can't you and Austin just get together during the day tomorrow?" *So that I don't have to babysit you?*

"Why can't we do both things?" said Sydney perkily. "We could all hang out at the mall tomorrow morning and then all hang out at the fair tomorrow night. Tyler could come to the mall too."

Only Austin and Tyler were still there. Bored with this conversation, Allie, Will, and even Danielle had wandered off. Now Austin glanced over at Tyler. "What do you think?"

Tyler was looking at the ground. "I guess we could do that."

"Yeah, okay. Sure," Austin told Sydney. It seemed to Gabby that he was speaking halfheartedly, but Sydney didn't notice.

"Perfect! Let's meet under the big clock in the food court at eleven. No, ten. Right when the mall opens."

"Sounds good," said Tyler. For some reason, he sounded about as enthusiastic as if he were going to the dentist. Maybe he liked sleeping late in the summer.

Gabby was almost hopping, she was so impatient. "Okay, okay! We'll see you tomorrow morning," she said. "But right now, we have to run. And I mean *run*."

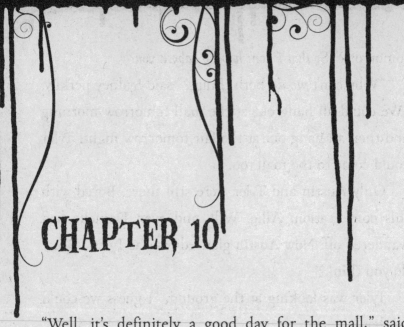

CHAPTER 10

"Well, it's definitely a good day for the mall," said Mrs. Costa, peering through the windshield at the fog. "Pretty soggy out there."

"I think it's a *beautiful* day," Sydney gushed. "This is my favorite kind of weather."

Her mom glanced at her in the rearview mirror. "Aren't we in a good mood this morning? Gabby, do you also love rainy days?"

"I don't know. I don't really think about the weather that much." Gabby was trying not to sound grumpy. Sydney had bounced awake at six that morning, all ready to talk about what she should wear to the mall. For Gabby, watching her try on a million shirts—and giving an opinion on each one—seemed like a terrible reason to get out of bed. And now it was drizzling out. Perfect!

When they passed the old highway, Gabby glanced out the window. She could just make out the fairground—as gray and ratty-looking as the day itself. Secretly, she was hoping that the rain would keep up all day. Wouldn't the fair have to be canceled if it was wet out? And even if it stopped raining, Sydney might not feel like tramping through a muddy cornfield.

"Is this a good mall we're going to?" she asked, trying to raise her spirits.

Sydney nodded excitedly. "It's great. It's way bigger than anything in San Francisco. It has every store in the world."

Gabby couldn't help smiling at that. "Wow. That *is* big."

"Maybe we won't feel like shopping, though. Maybe we'll just feel like—you know—walking around. Taking in the sights." Sydney gave Gabby a meaningful look.

"What sights would those be?" asked Mrs. Costa.

"The people! Maybe we'll just feel like people-watching." Again Sydney stared meaningfully at Gabby.

I get it, I get it, Gabby thought. *We are not going to the mall to shop.*

She sighed. It was occurring to her again that Sydney might have changed over the past year. Of course Sydney couldn't have stayed exactly the same as when she'd left—but the way she was acting around Austin had Gabby worrying that she might have changed enough to stop seeming like a best friend. Which was a sad thought to have, especially when there were still five days left of Gabby's visit. How was she going to get through them if Sydney kept being so gushy and love-struck?

Sydney's mom was pulling into the mall parking lot now, so Gabby decided to put the whole thing out of her mind. "Give me a call when you want to be picked up," Mrs. Costa said. "And have a great time."

"Thanks, Mom. I *know* we will," said Sydney.

An hour later, she wasn't nearly as optimistic.

Right at ten, the girls had parked themselves under the big clock in the food court. No one was there.

"Of course not!" Sydney said confidently. "The mall just opened. No one gets to a mall right when it opens." Gabby didn't point out that that was exactly what *they* had done.

Only three or four shoppers had passed when Sydney pulled out her phone.

"Seven minutes after ten. Boys are always late, I bet. Or maybe my phone is fast." She checked the big clock overhead, and her shoulders sagged a little. "No, it's right on time."

At 10:20, Gabby had suggested that they get something to eat. "We *are* in the food court," she pointed out. "We might as well do something to pass the time."

"No." Sydney's voice was tense. "I mean, you can get something if you feel like it. I don't want to miss them."

It had been 10:31 when Gabby returned with her smoothie, and Sydney was still standing alone.

"I hope nothing happened to them on the way," she fretted. "With all this rain, cars can skid or—or . . . sometimes they even have to pull over for a few minutes until it's not coming down as hard."

At ten forty-five, Gabby had gently asked if Sydney wanted to go shopping.

"No. I already told you that! Let's just give them a little bit longer. They may have thought I meant eleven. I did say eleven at first."

Now, at 11:06, Gabby announced that it was time to stop waiting.

Sydney's chin was trembling. "What if the boys got

the time wrong? We could stay here for a few more—"

"No," said Gabby firmly. "Even if they did come now, we'd look too desperate standing here."

"But Austin would never forget something this important!"

"I don't want to sound like your mom," said Gabby, "but you've known Austin for less than a day. We don't really know anything about him or Tyler."

"You can learn that a person's your soul mate in one minute," Sydney argued. "I *know* Austin. He wouldn't stand me up!"

Soul mate. Gabby was careful not to show how dumb she thought that was. "Then something's happened to keep the boys from getting here. Whatever it is, we'll go crazy if we wait any longer. Come on—let's go shopping."

There were tears in Sydney's eyes. "I don't want to go shopping. I just want to go home. I'm calling my mom to pick us up."

As soon as they were home, Sydney decided to go back to bed. "I'm going to pull the covers over my head and never think about anything again."

Gabby thought Sydney was making way too big a deal out of this, but at the same time she was sorry for her friend. Sydney was really upset. Still, Gabby didn't see why she should be bored during Sydney's nap. "Can I use your laptop while you're asleep?" she asked.

"You can use my laptop and my phone and my bike and anything you want. Just let me get some sleep."

Gabby had a private reason for borrowing the laptop. She wanted to do some research on the fair, and there hadn't been a chance until now. She took Sydney's laptop into the dining room and started searching. It seemed weird that typing in "Trouble Slope Fair" didn't turn anything up, but she knew that the contents of old newspapers didn't always show up the way newer stuff did. She did a quick search for the newspapers that seemed the closest to Trouble Slope—luckily, there were only three—and began skimming through everything from 1950 on.

The *Daily Standard* didn't say anything about the fair, and neither did the *Monroe County Gazette*. But with the third paper, the *Trouble Slope Times*, Gabby struck gold. The *Times* was a weekly paper that ran mostly feel-good stories about the town—stuff about kittens in trees and apple pie sales in front of the grocery store. In the March 17, 1953 edition, a headline at the bottom of the front page read: NEW FAIR COMING TO TOWN!

Gabby gave a sigh of relief. She'd been just about to give up the search.

"When the Iowa State Fair was moved to Des Moines, many children in this area were saddened," the article began. "No more Ferris wheel and roller coaster rides. No more Tunnel of Love. Not even a merry-go-round for tots."

I hate the word "tots," Gabby thought.

"But then Claudius the Magnificent—who refuses to give his last name—decided that the kids of Trouble Slope needed a fair of their own. Not a carnival that would come and go, but a fair that stayed open all summer. . . ."

Gabby had been so busy checking for headlines that she hadn't looked at any pictures. Now, glancing at the photo that went with the article, she gasped.

"Generous benefactor Claudius stands next to the new Ferris wheel," the caption read. And the man in the picture looked exactly like the magician painted on the fun house.

Well, not exactly. He wasn't wearing the magician

costume. But Gabby was absolutely sure that the painting had been modeled on this man.

The article went on to say that the carnival was expected to be ready by the summer of that same year. "Claudius will spare no expense to build a top-notch amusement park in record time."

"Record time" didn't sound that great to Gabby. Wouldn't it make more sense to take a *long* time building a top-notch amusement park? The next article she found seemed to answer yes to that question. It was from 1961, and it described a "minor accident" on the roller coaster when one of the cars had lost a wheel and fallen off the track.

"That's *minor?*" Gabby said aloud. But it turned out that no one had been riding on the roller coaster at the time. The car had fallen off in the night and been discovered the next morning. The fair was closed for three days for repairs and a full inspection.

The inspectors hadn't caught everything, though. Four years later, a man had been hurt when the Caterpillar ride stopped suddenly in mid-spin. He had survived the accident, but he later sued Claudius and won a lot of money.

A 1967 headline showed that the fair was still in trouble.

MOTHERS STAGE PROTEST AT FAIR—CLAIM RIDES UNSAFE

The photo showed a group of stern-looking women gathered in front of the Ferris wheel. The caption underneath read, "A boycott waiting to happen? These mothers are ready to take whatever action is needed."

After that, the *Trouble Slope Times* seemed to stop covering the fair. Maybe it had been too depressing for such an upbeat newspaper.

Gabby clicked off the laptop and stared into space, thinking. The articles might explain why the fair had fallen into such decay. But they didn't begin to explain how it could have been resurrected for Kids' Week. . . .

While Gabby was still pondering this, Sydney came into the room—or, more accurately, burst in. Her eyes were shining, and her face was pink with excitement. "I feel so much better!" she said happily. "I'm all ready for the fair tonight."

"*What?* You still want to go?"

Sydney looked surprised. "Sure, why not? We told Austin and Tyler we'd be there."

"You want to see them even after they stood us up this morning?"

"I'm positive they didn't mean to," said Sydney. "And I have to know what happened. Come *on*, Gabby! Don't be such a party pooper!"

"It's not because of the boys that I don't want to go," Gabby confessed. "I mean, that's part of it. But the real thing is . . . well . . . I think the fair is kind of creepy."

She hadn't planned to tell Sydney about the way the painting of Claudius had winked at her the night before. It sounded too crazy. Now, suddenly, she found herself sharing the story. "I just don't know if I can handle going back," she finished. "Plus, I read about the fair online. A lot of bad things happened there."

Sydney was staring at her. "It's not that I don't believe you," she finally said. "But it's not like you to freak out about something like this. You're the adventurous one, remember? Gabby, I *know* you know that the painting couldn't have winked at you. It must have been a shadow or something." Then, seeing Gabby's face, she added, "But if you start feeling weird again

tonight, we'll leave right away. I promise."

Gabby had been pretty sure Sydney wouldn't give in. And at least the sun was shining again. If the good weather kept up, they wouldn't have to sit on wet rides in the rain.

"Maybe we could do some kind of non-fair thing this afternoon," she suggested.

"Good idea! For starters, we can plan what we're going to wear to the fair tonight."

Gabby groaned. "I meant something like watching a movie. Or going swimming or doing a craft. You know—an activity." Privately, she was thinking that even helping Sydney's parents with chores would be more interesting than talking about what to wear.

And she, Gabby, had started all this! If she hadn't made such a fuss, she and Sydney would never have gone to the fairground in the first place.

At least this was the last night of the fair. Once it was over, maybe she and Sydney could go back to the way they'd been before.

If that was even possible . . .

"You came right on time!" Austin rushed up and gave Sydney a big hug. The girls had tracked down Austin, Tyler, and the three other kids on the midway. "That's so great!"

"Well, you didn't come at all," said Gabby. "Where were you guys this morning?"

Both boys looked sheepish. "We should have checked first," Austin told her. "It turned out that my mom couldn't drive us after all."

Sydney had looked a little wary, but now she relaxed. "I knew it wasn't your fault," she said, giving Gabby an *I told you so* look. "Let's exchange phone numbers right now."

"I don't have any paper," said Austin.

Sydney frowned. "We can do it on our phones!" She pulled hers out of her pocket and waved it in his face. "Remember phones?"

"*That's* a phone?" said Tyler incredulously. Then he seemed to catch himself. "It's just that I've never seen one that's so . . . so . . ." He seemed to be hunting for a word. "So fancy. My phone's not like that."

Austin cleared his throat uncomfortably. "Mine isn't either. Anyway, let's figure out phone numbers later." In a mock-suave voice, he added, "For the night, she is still young."

"Plus, my parents said we could stay until eleven," Sydney told him. "Because it's the last night and everything. So we have even more time than you thought!"

All the games were up and running, with crowds of kids lined up to play them. Looking around her, Gabby started to feel better. The rain had left the whole fairground even more clean and sparkling than it had been the night before. Now the early-evening sun was lending a golden, mellow glow to the scene. Everything was going to be okay after all.

"Hey, Sydney, see that big pink teddy bear in the bottle-toss booth?" asked Austin. "I'm going to win it for you. Let's go!" He grabbed Sydney's hand, and the two of them headed down to the game. The rest of the group followed more slowly.

Danielle's mood hadn't improved overnight. As they all strolled along, Gabby saw her nudge Will and point at Sydney. "It's too easy with some of them," she said.

"What do you mean?" asked Gabby.

At the same time, Tyler snapped, "Shut up, Danielle. Just shut up." Turning to Gabby, he said, "Want to try this?"

"This" was a game called Racetrack. Eight small

plastic horses were lined up at one end of the booth. By aiming streams of water at the buttons underneath the horses, players could make the horses wobble along toward the other side of the booth.

"Oh, I'm no good at shooting games," said Gabby.

"This isn't really *shooting* shooting," said Tyler. "All you have to do is point the spray at your horse and let the water do the work for you. Right, Mosby?"

Mosby, it seemed, was the name of the dark-haired carny who kept showing up everywhere.

"Right, Tyler," Mosby replied. "The game plays itself. Which horse do you want, miss?"

"Green, I guess."

"Okay, I'll take the red one," said Tyler.

"I'll be purple," Allie chimed in.

The three of them positioned themselves in front of the huge water pistols fastened to the counter. When Mosby switched the bell on, they pumped the triggers on their pistols as hard as they could. Tyler's and Allie's horses moved forward smoothly, but the pistols were heavy and hard to steer, and Gabby had trouble getting the green horse to budge. "I told you I couldn't do it," she complained as her horse quivered in place. "It just looks as if I'm giving him a bath!"

"Pull harder," urged Tyler. For some reason, he glanced over at Mosby as he spoke.

Gabby was already pulling the trigger as hard as she could, but suddenly the green horse shot out ahead of the other two. Swiftly and smoothly it rushed across the booth to cross the finish line. Another bell rang, and the word WINNER flashed on and off at the top of the booth.

"How did that happen?" said Gabby. "I thought these games were rigged to make people *lose*."

"Of course they're not," said Tyler. "You were just good at it, that's all. Which prize do you want?"

"I don't need a prize," Gabby said. Secretly, she was thinking that all the prizes looked pretty tacky. But Mosby reached into a barrel of stuffed animals and held out a blue stuffed giraffe with a flourish.

"Congratulations," he said. Then his expression changed. "Is there something wrong?"

Gabby was staring at the giraffe. She was sure she had seen it before, that first afternoon at the fair. It had been lying in a puddle at the abandoned fairground. It had been faded and torn then, but now it was brand-new.

What was going on here?

"You don't like the giraffe?" asked Mosby anxiously. "I can get you a different prize."

Gabby gave herself a little shake. There was no way she could possibly explain any of this—and no reason to hurt the carny's feelings. "I love the giraffe!" she said, putting as much feeling into her voice as she could. "It just reminded me of something, that's all."

"Are your stomachs settled?" asked Tyler. "Because this ride is famous for making people throw up."

"I don't get sick on rides!" Gabby said indignantly. "I suppose there's always a first time, but I'm not worried."

"I am," said Sydney. "I still think I should sit this one out."

But Austin wouldn't hear of it. "You won't be scared with me," he said confidently. "I'll distract you."

The four of them had gotten some ice cream and played a few more games. Gabby had won three and Sydney had won two. Sometime between Gabby's second and third wins, Danielle had rolled her eyes and left, taking Will and Allie with her. Gabby couldn't say she was sorry to see her go.

But something had to be going on! Some of these games, Gabby knew, were impossible for *anyone* to win. They'd been built that way. The Balloon and Dart game looked easy enough. Passersby were supposed to see it and think, *How hard could it be to pop a balloon by throwing a dart at it?* After all, the balloons were only about six feet away. But you could throw a dart from one foot away and not pop a balloon—if the end of the dart was dull and the balloon hadn't been fully inflated.

And yet, on her very first try, Sydney had popped all five balloons in a row. In the ring toss game, Gabby had somehow managed to throw a ring over each one of the bowling pins lined up in front of her. The girls had had the same luck with each game they tried.

Maybe Mosby had been fixing the games to give them an unfair advantage. He might have thought it was a nice thing to do. But to Gabby, it was just weird. She had finally suggested that they take a ride on the Tilt-A-Whirl.

The ride had seven bubble-shaped cars that were fastened onto a rotating platform. "As soon as things speed up, the operator will start raising and lowering the platform in sections," Tyler explained to Sydney. "That will make the cars spin around in different directions—sometimes slowly, sometimes fast. There's no way to predict which direction they'll spin in or how fast they'll go. It's got something to do with centrifugal force, but that's all I know."

"Promise me again that none of us will fly off into the air," said Sydney for about the tenth time as she and Austin climbed into a car across from the one Gabby and Tyler had chosen.

"There's no way we can," Austin assured her. "We'll be pressed against the back of the car. And there's a lap bar."

Mosby, the carny, was the operator on the Tilt-A-Whirl. (*Who else*, thought Gabby.) He made a quick inspection of each car, checking that the bars were secure and locking the doors.

"You can slow this down if we ask you to, right?" asked Sydney. Again, it was not the first time she had asked this.

"Absolutely," Mosby assured her. "Just give me a signal and I'll take it way down. I don't want anyone getting sick—I'm the one who has to wash the cars."

"Mosby's the best ride operator, though," Tyler put in. "He knows how to make this ride totally unpredictable.

It's almost as if he can turn gravity on and off."

"Oh, great," moaned Sydney.

"No, no, I mean it in a good way!" said Tyler quickly. He turned to Gabby. "This is going to be the best Tilt-A-Whirl ride you've ever been on."

For a couple of moments, the car just swung around in lazy half circles. As the platform began rising and falling, then spinning faster and faster, the cars themselves began to whirl.

Gabby was having a great time. It felt almost like a boat riding ocean swells. When the car stopped suddenly and began spinning in the opposite direction, she felt as if she were weightless for a second. Mosby reversed the direction of the entire ride, making their car race backward, and Gabby beamed at Tyler. "This is great!" she yelled.

They were about to pass Mosby at the controls. Just as they drew level with him, Tyler yelled, "Mosby! Go faster!"

Mosby grinned and gave them a thumbs-up sign.

The whirling platform picked up speed. Gabby couldn't help screaming with laughter. The faster it went, the harder she laughed, and the harder she laughed, the more she screamed. And the more she screamed, the faster the ride moved. In a few seconds, they were spinning so rapidly that Gabby couldn't see anything except colors.

Wait. That wasn't supposed to be happening. The Tilt-A-Whirl couldn't possibly be meant to go *this* fast!

"It's too much!" she called to Tyler.

He grinned back at her. "Yeah, isn't it great?"

"No, I mean it's too fast!"

"Can't hear you!" Tyler yelled back.

Gabby blinked hard, trying to focus. Where was Mosby? She had to get his attention. Their part of the platform was high in the air now, and she could see right down to the controls.

But Mosby's chair was empty. He wasn't at the controls. Gabby couldn't see him anywhere.

And the ride was still picking up speed.

Gabby was screaming with pure terror now. Their car was shaking so hard she was worried that it might fly apart.

In a few seconds, they would be thrown out of the car . . . it was just spinning too fast. And at this speed, who knew if they would survive. . . .

CHAPTER 11

Gabby was screaming too hysterically to notice that Tyler was shaking her by the shoulder. "Don't worry, Gabby! I see Mosby! I'll make him stop!" he said. He leaned out as far as he could and signaled frantically. In a few seconds, the sickening angle of the car straightened out, and the Tilt-A-Whirl began to slow down.

"I'm really sorry," said Tyler as the ride gradually came to a stop. "I thought you were having fun. I wouldn't have asked Mosby to spin us faster if I'd known it would scare you so much."

Gabby's heart was still pounding, and she hadn't quite gotten her breath back. "It—it wasn't that it was going so fast," she said. "It's that Mosby left the ride. His seat was empty. Didn't you notice?"

When Gabby stood up, her legs were so wobbly that it was hard to walk. Tyler put his hand under her elbow to steady her as they walked down the ramp.

He pointed at Mosby, who gave them a little wave. "There he is. Right where he always was. You didn't leave during the ride, did you?" he asked the carny.

Mosby looked shocked. "Of course not! That would be way too dangerous. We're not allowed to go anywhere while a ride's in progress."

"That's good." Gabby's voice was shaking. "But I have to talk to Sydney for a second." Without waiting for Tyler, she pushed her way through the crowd.

Sydney and Austin were far ahead. Hand in hand, they were walking toward the Ferris wheel. Gabby picked up her pace.

"What's your hurry?" Tyler's voice came from behind her. "Is something wrong?"

"No, no," Gabby said over her shoulder. "I just need to talk to her, that's all."

Tyler laughed. "I don't think they're going anywhere. Look how long the line is!"

He was right. Sydney and Austin had just joined

Will and Allie at the end of a very long line. They hadn't moved by the time Gabby reached them.

"Syd! Hi. Can I talk to you for a second?"

"Sure! What's up?"

"I mean in private. Just for a second."

"Oh—well, okay." Sydney turned to Austin. "Will you please save my place?" she asked.

"No, really, what's up?" she asked again as she and Gabby walked away from the line.

"Can we go home now?"

Sydney looked shocked. "What are you talking about? Austin and I still haven't gone on the Ferris wheel." She gestured toward the line. "You can see for yourself that it's going to take ages."

"I know, but remember how you said we could go home if I was feeling weird? Well, I *am* feeling weird. That ride was too much for me."

Sydney frowned. "What do you mean? I liked it."

"You *liked* that ride? I mean, *you* liked it?"

"I'm not a baby, you know." Sydney's voice had sharpened. "Not *everything* scares me."

"But—but that ride was horrible! You had to have noticed that something was wrong. I thought our car was going to come unhooked. And Mosby left the controls halfway through the ride!"

Sydney shrugged. "That didn't happen to our car. We had a nice smooth ride, and it wasn't too fast at all. I don't know what you're talking about."

"Maybe the cars run at different speeds, then," said Gabby. "All I know is that in our car, it was really, really bad. I want to leave. I've had enough of this fair."

"I haven't," said Sydney simply.

Gabby couldn't believe what she was hearing. "You *said* we could go home whenever I wanted," she repeated. "You promised!"

"Yes, but I figured you'd have a good time once we got here. Look around, everyone else is."

"Sydney—" Gabby made a helpless gesture. "I can't go back alone. And it will be eleven soon, anyway."

"Forget about the curfew," Sydney snapped. "And stop pretending to be a grown-up. You're not in charge here. I'm staying, no matter what you say."

Before Gabby could answer, Sydney had turned and flounced back to her place in line next to Austin.

Slowly Gabby walked over to Tyler. "I can't believe it. She—she doesn't care about anything but Austin. I don't think she's ever disobeyed her parents before."

Tyler didn't look too concerned. "So she blew you off! It's not the end of the world."

No, Gabby wanted to say. *But it might be the end of a friendship.*

"Forget Sydney," Tyler continued. "Let's go on another ride."

Gabby groaned. "I don't think I can handle another ride."

"Why don't you go on the Tunnel of Love?" came a voice from behind Gabby. A cool, sarcastic voice. Gabby turned and—of course—saw Danielle. *Just what I needed,* she thought drearily.

"The Tunnel of Love is *very* romantic," Danielle went on snidely.

I won't let her get to me, Gabby promised herself. In her sweetest voice, she said, "What a great idea, Danielle! I'm sure we'll love it. Tyler, let's hurry over there!"

She grabbed Tyler by the arm and practically yanked him along with her, leaving Danielle standing on the sidewalk. She looked incredibly worried at the thought of Gabby and Tyler going into the Tunnel of Love together. *Well, you suggested it,* thought Gabby crossly.

"What was *that* about?" asked Tyler once they were walking normally again.

"Oh, nothing. Being supersweet was the only way I could think of to deal with her. But I'm actually fine with going on the Tunnel of Love. It isn't like a real ride—it's not going to fall off the rails or anything."

Gabby had never been on a Tunnel of Love ride before. She had vaguely imagined that it involved heart-shaped cars, but she hadn't thought about the "tunnel" part. So she was a little disappointed to see that the Tunnel of Love was not one of the better-looking rides at this fair. It was a long, winding, tunnel-shaped building painted a garish pink that showed all its stains. A smelly black liquid as opaque as paint filled a stone channel that led into the tunnel.

And the boats! They were supposed to be gondolas, but Gabby could see that they were only pink rowboats with some intricate but worn-down carving on the front. The paddles in the oarlocks were pink too—at least their handles were. Their blades had turned a dirty gray.

"Maybe this is a scary ride after all," Gabby said. She pointed at the black liquid in the channel. "What's that?"

Tyler chuckled. "Believe it or not, it's water—probably

the same water they've used since the fair opened."

Gabby could believe him. A ton of trash was floating in the channel. A broken Styrofoam cooler. Some empty cans of something called New Coke. (New Coke—what was that?) There was even a crumpled old record sleeve. Gabby only recognized *that* because her grandfather had kept all his old vinyl records. There was also plenty of garbage that Gabby didn't recognize and didn't want to.

She shuddered as she looked down at their boat. Its padded seat had been ripped out by either vandals or animals. "Do we really have to go on this?"

"Oh, come on. It's fun once you get into the tunnel. Everyone should ride this at least once." Tyler bowed and offered Gabby his arm fake-gallantly. "May I assist you, mademoiselle?—Wait, let me get aboard first," he added in his normal voice. He clambered into the boat and held out his hand.

Gabby hesitated. "What if I fall into that gross water?"

"I won't let that happen. You're safe with me."

Gabby stepped reluctantly into the rickety boat.

Then they sat there.

"Is this all?" Gabby asked after a minute.

"It'll start on its own." As if to prove that Tyler was

right, a grinding mechanical noise started somewhere in the tunnel. The boat jerked. Then it began to glide forward.

What struck Gabby was how quiet the whole thing was. Once the boat began to move, it didn't make a sound. She pulled at an oar to see what would happen. A smell of something rotten wafted up, and Gabby hastily dropped the oar.

They were almost in the tunnel now. As the boat drifted up to the entrance, Gabby could see that dingy plastic swans had been fastened to the walls just above water level. Above the swans, plastic Cupids were holding up giant pink plastic hearts. Above the Cupids were a few battered silver stars and two crescent moons—on each wall of the tunnel.

"Danielle was right," Gabby said sarcastically. "This *is* romantic."

"It's kind of cruddy-looking," Tyler agreed. "That doesn't matter much—no one can see it once they're inside. The lights have been broken for a while. But it's still fun."

When the whole boat was in the tunnel, Gabby saw what he meant—about the dark part, at least. The tunnel was absolutely black except for a few cracks in the ceiling that let in thin lines of light. From some hidden sound system, creepy old-time violins were playing. It was just about the least fun place she could imagine.

"I'm not sure that even Sydney and Austin would like this," she said. "I wish the boat would go faster. It's *crawling* along."

"Hey, why are you in such a bad mood?" asked Tyler. "You don't like the Tunnel of Love, you don't like the Tilt-A-Whirl, you don't like the roller coaster, you don't like this, you don't like that. Why did you come back today if you hate the fair so much?"

"Sydney made me," Gabby blurted before she realized how rude it sounded. "I'm sorry, but that's why." At this point, she might as well be honest. "There's something wrong with this fair. A lot of things, actually."

"Wrong? What do you mean?"

"Well, I've seen what it looks like in the daytime."

She could feel Tyler freeze next to her. "You've seen it in the daytime," he repeated.

"Yes. Sydney and I checked it out yesterday afternoon, and it was just a pile of junk. Worse than junk. How did it get all cleaned up that night?"

Tyler shrugged. "How should I know? They probably had a lot of people working on it."

"I don't think so. Because that reminds me of something else: Why is Mosby the only guy working here?"

"What are you talking about? Are you still upset about the Tilt-A-Whirl?"

"It's not just the Tilt-A-Whirl! Mosby was the only guy running the games. And last night he sold me some cotton candy *and* operated the roller coaster."

"So maybe they're understaffed."

"Understaffed enough to have only one worker? That doesn't make any sense!" Gabby could feel herself getting fired up. "And what's the deal with that stupid space ride? Don't you realize how outdated it is? And why don't any of you have phones? And why do you all wear watches when *no one* our age wears a watch?"

There was a silence of perhaps a minute before Tyler answered. It was too dark to see his face, but Gabby could hear the edge in his voice. "You know, you're pretty observant for someone your age."

"*My* age?" exclaimed Gabby. "We're the same age! Or pretty much the same. How old are you exactly?"

"I've been around longer than you have." Now Tyler

sounded sad. "A lot longer." He sighed. "I guess it's time to let you know what's going on."

"I'm listening," said Gabby.

"Well, this fair was started in the early 1950s—"

"I know," Gabby interrupted. "I read about it this afternoon."

"Okay, then you know that the guy who founded it was named Claudius the Magnificent. Claudius loved kids. He started out as a small-time magician. He did birthday parties, things like that. Then he inherited some money and decided to build a fair. He wanted to make a lot of kids happy, not just a few. And for a long time, it worked."

The boat slid around a bend. There was still no light ahead. *This is a long ride,* Gabby thought.

Tyler continued. "Things started going south for Claudius in the 1970s. Kids were more interested in TV and movies than in his fair. Then there were a couple of accidents on worn-out rides. Claudius didn't have the money to make repairs, and he got a lot of bad press. Finally the fair was shut down. The closed-down, abandoned fair is what you saw in the afternoon."

He paused for so long that finally Gabby had to prompt

him. "Okay, the fair closed. Then why is it open tonight?"

"Claudius arranged that." Again Tyler paused. "You remember that I said he was a magician?"

"Yes. What does that have to do with anything?"

"He was a real magician."

"You already said that! What does it have to do with—" Then Gabby realized what Tyler meant.

"Wait a second. You're not saying—you're not saying Claudius used magic to start up the fair again?"

"Yes. That's what I'm saying."

"Oh, come on. There's no such thing as magic."

"*Then how did I get here?*"

"What—what are you talking about?"

"I'm talking about the spell Claudius cast. The spell that opens the fair for just seven nights a year, from eight till midnight."

"Kids' Week," Gabby whispered.

"That's right. And why is it called Kids' Week? Because it's the week that Claudius collects kids. On the last night of every Kids' Week, anyone who's still here at midnight stays here. Permanently."

Gabby groaned. "Okay, you got me. I was actually starting to believe you."

"It's the *truth*. I know it is, because he collected me," Tyler said bitterly. "I've been here for more than thirty years. I'll be a kid at this fair until the end of time."

He gripped Gabby's shoulder so hard that it hurt. "Don't you tell me there's no magic. I know better. So does Austin. And so do the rest of my friends."

"Wait. Austin and Danielle and—"

"All of us," Tyler said. "And a lot more."

All of a sudden, Gabby had the sick feeling that he was telling the truth. It would explain so many of the things that had been bothering her. "Is that why you don't have cell phones?" she asked.

"If you mean that thing you have, then no. The last phone I ever used plugged into the wall."

"And that's why you didn't show up at the mall. You can never leave the fair."

"Right. One summer night, thirty years ago, I was playing a pinball game in the arcade. I wanted to finish it, so I stayed a couple of minutes past closing time. And—like I said—any kid who's still on the grounds at midnight is trapped here forever."

At that moment, their boat came to a creaking halt.

"It always stops halfway through the ride," Tyler told

her. The matter-of-fact way he said it was as scary as everything else he'd been saying. How horrible to be trapped at a fair for so long that you got to know every detail of every ride.

Speaking of trapped . . .

Gabby realized that she didn't know what time it was. How long had she and Tyler been sitting on this boat, anyway? She started to reach for her phone.

"What are you doing?" asked Tyler sharply.

"I—I'm checking the time."

"Oh, don't bother," said Tyler. "My watch glows in the dark." He checked it, then held out his wrist for her to see.

"It's a quarter to twelve," he said.

Only fifteen minutes until closing time! Gabby couldn't believe it. "We've got to get off this ride so I can find Sydney!" she cried.

But Tyler only leaned back in the seat and yawned.

"There's no hurry," he said lazily. "You're not going anywhere. You're staying right here with me until midnight.

"And then you'll be here forever. Just like me."

"Wait," Gabby said desperately. "You don't mean that. You don't want to keep *me* here."

Tyler laughed. "What are you talking about? Of course I do! It gets so boring here without new people. We can never convince anyone to stay until midnight. You and Sydney are the first in a very long time."

Gabby screamed.

"No one can hear you," Tyler said calmly.

"*Help!*" Gabby shrieked again. "Please, someone, help me!"

"Shut up!" Tyler hissed. He lunged toward her in the dark and grabbed her arm.

Still screaming, Gabby fumbled for the oar with her other hand. She couldn't break it out of the oarlock, but she could pull the handle toward her. And she did. As hard as she could, she yanked the oar across her body and jabbed Tyler in the side with it. He yelped with pain and surprise—and let go of her arm. In that instant, Gabby scrambled over the side of the boat.

"Hey!" Tyler yelled. "Get back here!" But Gabby was already splashing ahead toward the exit.

The lukewarm water only reached her knees. It felt horribly oily, and she could feel her legs brushing against soft, anonymous things suspended in the murk. But she pushed on. Behind her, she heard Tyler jump out of the boat.

He must have slipped as he landed, because Gabby heard a big splash. Then he was on his feet again. She could hear the water swooshing as his legs moved.

Tyler's fall had bought her a few extra seconds. But he was taller than she was, plus he knew every inch of this place. *He'll catch up for sure,* Gabby thought. Where, where was the exit?

With a small, distant part of her brain, she realized that "the light at the end of the tunnel" wasn't just an expression. That light was all she wanted now! She rounded a bend and almost collapsed with relief. There *was* light ahead. The shining lights of the fair. She was reaching the end. If only she could get there before Tyler caught her . . .

Gabby had been concentrating on the sounds behind her. All that mattered to her was that Tyler could not— *must not*—catch her.

It had never occurred to her to worry about what lay ahead. She hadn't considered the possibility that someone might be waiting for her.

Which was why she was totally unprepared when she crashed full-force into the dark figure at the end of the tunnel.

CHAPTER 12

The person clapped a hand over Gabby's mouth before she could make a sound. She was pushed, stumbling, toward the end of the tunnel, and then the person whispered, "It's Danielle. When we get outside, hide behind the food stand on your left." Then Gabby felt the rough edge of the tunnel scrape against her ankle. "Now! Go," commanded Danielle.

Gabby didn't stop to think. She hurled herself across the twenty feet between the end of the tunnel and the food stand. Then she ducked behind it, saw a ledge made by the counter, and crouched underneath. Danielle was right on her heels. The two of them squatted side by side, trying to breathe as quietly as they could. Had Tyler spotted them?

The two or three minutes the girls hid seemed like forever to Gabby. It was strange to see the fairgoers strolling around as if nothing was the matter. Now Gabby noticed that all of them were dressed like Danielle and Tyler. Was everyone here trapped? Were she and Sydney the only ones still able to leave?

At last Danielle murmured, "I think he's gone."

"Thank you," Gabby said fervently.

"Shh! You can't let anyone know I helped you, or I'll be in big trouble."

"Why did you help me? I thought you hated me!"

"No! You seem nice," said Danielle. "I was hoping that if I was nasty enough, you would stay away from the fair. I *hate* it when kids get trapped here. I wanted to tell you to leave right away, but if I did . . . let's just say things would get even worse for me. But now you've got to get out of here. There's not much time left."

"I can't leave without Sydney!" whispered Gabby.

Danielle's voice was tight with strain. "I can't help you anymore. I can't let anyone see us together. Good luck—and I'm sorry about everything."

As Gabby huddled under the counter, Danielle stood

up cautiously, darted a look around her, and then sprinted away. When she was out of sight, Gabby jumped to her feet. She didn't even bother to look around. She took off in the direction of the Ferris wheel, racing as fast as she could.

It wasn't as fast as she wanted. Her legs were cramped and aching, and she kept stumbling. She felt as if she'd been running for her entire life. A few people eyed her curiously as she rushed by, but Gabby didn't care. All she could think about was the Ferris wheel. Was Sydney still there?

Now the Ferris wheel was dead ahead of her. It looked eerily beautiful as it turned slowly against the dark sky. Every car was full. Gabby could make out the silhouettes of couples, singles, and groups of friends. And as she got nearer, she saw that there was still a line of kids waiting to ride.

Her heart leaped with hope. Maybe Sydney was still in the line. Or was that Sydney and Austin at the head of the line right now? Yes, it was! Gabby pounded toward them, straining to call Sydney's name. But her voice came out as a croaking wheeze, and Sydney didn't turn around.

Fifty yards to go. Then ten. And then Gabby had reached the end of the line. Without thinking she began pushing her way through the waiting people.

"Hey!" someone yelled as Gabby squeezed by. "You can't do that!"

Gabby didn't care how rude she seemed. She only wanted to reach Sydney. She shoved two indignant teenagers out of the way, scrambled past a girl holding her little brother's hand . . . and realized that Sydney's car was just leaving the ground.

Gabby cupped her mouth with her hands and screamed with every bit of strength she had left. *"Syd! Sydney!"* But she didn't have a chance against the rollicking music of the Ferris wheel. And Sydney, leaning her head against Austin's shoulder, was oblivious to everything else in the world.

Austin had spotted Gabby, though. As he slid his arm around Sydney's shoulders, he shot a mocking, triumphant smile Gabby's way.

Gabby had no breath left. Panting, she leaned forward to rest her hands on her knees. The ride's cheerful tune seemed like mockery as it floated out into the dark. "You'll NEV-er reach her! You'll NEV-er reach her," it seemed to be saying. "Not EV-er ever ever ever ev—"

And then the Ferris wheel came to a halt.

The cars rocked gently in the air. Gabby could see that Sydney's and Austin's car was at the very top.

"*Sydney!*" she screamed again. She knew there was no chance that her voice would reach that high. She would have to try something else. *Something drastic this time,* she told herself.

Gabby flicked a glance over to the operator's booth. It was unmanned—no surprise there. Ignoring the shouts behind her, Gabby started to clamber over the security gate.

I'll bring Sydney down myself!

Just as she put one leg over the gate, she heard a man's voice.

"I wouldn't try that if I were you. It won't do any good."

Mosby, the carny, had come up beside her.

"Come on, get down from there," he said gently, holding out a hand to steady her.

Slowly Gabby climbed back down. The carny kept a hand on her shoulder as he turned to the line of people behind her.

"No one else gets on the ride tonight, folks. Closing time."

He looked down at Gabby. "You could leave too. You still have a little time."

"You're in on this, aren't you?" Gabby asked.

"Oh yes," said Mosby sadly. "Claudius was my uncle. He needed someone to keep an eye on things. So he . . . brought me in, I guess you'd say. But I won't stop you from leaving." He pointed. "There's an exit right over there."

Gabby sighed with relief. "Thank you. Thank you so much. I'll wait for Sydney, and then we can—"

"Oh, your friend won't be coming with you."

For an instant, his words made no sense. "*What? Why not? It would only take a second for you to bring her down!*"

"Can't do that, miss. A ride's a ride."

"But she doesn't know the rule about midnight. She'll be stuck here forever! Please, *please* bring her down!"

"A ride's a ride," the carny repeated. "She stood in line like everyone else. And I've got to give her the full ride that she waited for."

"No! This can't be happening!"

"The fair's about to close," Mosby reminded her. He

held out his wrist to show her his watch—an old-style watch, with a second hand that was almost at 11:59.

"Gabby!" came a ferocious shout. Tyler had finally found her. He was pounding toward the Ferris wheel, his face thunderous with rage.

The Ferris wheel's jaunty tune filtered through distant screams from the roller coaster.

The carny was still holding up his wrist for her to see. "One minute left," he warned.

Tyler had gotten so close that Gabby could hear his feet slamming against the pavement. *"Don't move!"* he yelled.

Gabby looked at Mosby's watch. Forty seconds left. She glanced up at Sydney. The exit was so close, and Sydney looked so very far away. . . .

Half a minute until midnight.

If she didn't run now, Tyler would catch her. If she left, she'd be abandoning her best friend.

Should she escape—and leave Sydney here forever?

Should she stay to be with Sydney—and never see the real world again?

There were twenty seconds left. . . .

EPILOGUE

An old Ferris wheel is a lonely sight at midnight.

Actually, this whole deserted fairground looks lonely tonight. A stray breeze stirs the dark, dirty water in the Tunnel of Love. A rusty old cotton-candy cart lies on its side, its wheels spinning. A crumpled flyer advertising Kids' Week blows across a path past the motionless Tilt-A-Whirl.

But somehow it's the Ferris wheel that looks the loneliest. Its lights were turned off years ago. The uppermost car sways slightly in the wind.

Wait. Is it really the wind that's moving that car?

Is someone screaming up there—a trapped passenger, maybe?

Of course not. No one is riding the Ferris wheel. You must have dreamed it.

Just the way you're now dreaming that you hear *two* people screaming. . . .

Let's get out of here. An old fairground is a dangerous place to visit.

DO NOT FEAR—
WE HAVE ANOTHER CREEPY TALE FOR YOU!

TURN THE PAGE FOR A SNEAK PEEK AT

You're invited to a

CREEPOVER®

The Terror Behind the Mask

Jasmine Porter always read before she went to sleep. It felt great to get into bed, turn on the reading light that was clipped to her headboard, and open a book. It was like entering another world. And she usually fell asleep while reading.

Tonight, Jasmine would start a book her dad had bought her on one of their father-daughter book-buying sprees before he went off on his latest trip. They always went to the same neighborhood bookstore, Bookworm, and her dad would always say the same thing: "Pick out what you want, Jazzy-Jas." And he really meant it. Jasmine could choose twenty books and her dad wouldn't even blink in surprise. He'd just smile, take them from her, and plop them down at the register.

"Really?" she'd sometimes say when she'd gone on a particularly large binge. "I can have all of those?"

And her dad would always say the same thing: "You can't put a price on the pleasure that reading gives."

It was true they both loved to read. Sometimes they would sit on the couch for hours, both immersed in their own book, and not say a word to each other. The only sound in the room would be of pages turning.

That's what it was like as Jasmine lay in bed reading, too. It was just her breathing and the sound of pages turning. The bulb of her reading lamp was so bright she could actually feel its heat. After a few chapters, Jasmine's eyes grew heavy, her grip on the book started to loosen, and she knew she should close it, turn off the reading light, put the book on the night table, and face the truth: she would finally have to give in to sleep.

Jasmine reached up and turned off the reading light, but instead of going dark, the room was still lit up. Jasmine looked up and noticed that the overhead light was still on. She dragged herself out of bed and walked, bleary-eyed, toward the light switch next to the door, and flicked the switch.

But as the room went dark, Jasmine quickly realized that she should have turned the reading light back on, because now it was pitch black in her room, unless you counted the glow-in-the-dark stars on her ceiling, which didn't exactly provide any real light (though they were pretty). Where was that little night-light that was plugged into the outlet? It usually gave off a soft glow all night long and made Jasmine feel so much better about being in the dark.

As much as she hated to admit it, Jasmine was afraid of the dark. And she really liked that night-light. It was made of orange and yellow glass and shaped like a baby owl, and she'd had it since she was a baby. *The bulb must've burned out,* she thought. The last few times that had happened, she'd called out to her dad, who would come in and change the bulb. But her dad was still away on his trip and Jasmine was alone in the house with her grandmother, and Jasmine knew Nana would already be asleep.

Jasmine sighed. It seemed like her dad was always gone at the wrong times.

Sometimes he would try to talk to her about his having to travel a lot for work, as if he was fishing for her real feelings about him being gone. "Did you have any dreams while I was gone?" he'd ask, as if that would give him some clue to her deepest thoughts. Or he'd say, "When I was your age, I hated it when my mom went back to work and left me home alone a lot." It was like he expected Jasmine to immediately join the conversation and confess her true feelings about it just being her and her grandmother a lot of the time.

And Jasmine just wasn't going to do that. She also wasn't going to tell her dad how scared she still was of the dark, or about the weird little rituals she believed kept her safe at night. For the past three years, she'd been whispering "you're okay" to herself three times and making sure the covers were pulled up all the way to her ears before she would close her eyes. And she wasn't going to tell him she thought that maybe he'd traveled the world enough, and that maybe it was time to stay put and be a real parent, like full-time, no joke.

So whenever he tried to start a conversation like this, Jasmine pretended she was someone else—someone who didn't care. And she'd shrug or roll her eyes.

Now Jasmine stood at the light switch. She could turn the overhead light back on, walk to the bed, turn on the reading light and then come back. But that would set her back from falling asleep. No, she could do this.

Jasmine tried to let her eyes adjust to the dark so she could see a tiny bit, just so she could make her way back to bed without tripping and falling on her face. And, of course, so that she could keep a close eye on the closet as she passed it. Because the idea of something being in that closet—something that was going to get her—was so real to Jasmine that she feared it deep in her bones.

"The Bogeyman" didn't quite do it justice, nor did "monster." Both names sounded childish compared to what she actually feared. Which, of course, she couldn't even name.

When she was younger, she'd make her dad check the closet before she went to sleep. He'd always reassure her that there was no such thing as the Bogeyman, and that there were no monsters in the closet. Jasmine's dad always humored her by opening it and looking around first. But now that she was older, she was embarrassed to ask him to check. Still, she was too afraid to check herself. Instead, she settled for staring at the closet door, making sure it didn't creak open and release some horrible, evil . . . thing.

The basic outline of the room was starting to reveal itself to Jasmine's tired, anxious eyes. The light creeping in from the hallway was helping a bit. Jasmine knew it was time to walk past the closet and jump quickly into bed. She tentatively crept forward, still afraid of tripping in her messy room. One foot in front of the other, one foot in front of the other, she chanted in her head. She kept her eyes on that closet door, as if by sheer will she could keep it closed and keep herself safe from whatever was inside.

It felt like forever, but Jasmine finally made to her bed. And there she was, standing at the side of her bed, ready to crawl under the covers to safety, when she felt it grab her, suddenly, around her left ankle.

WANT MORE CREEPINESS?

Then you're in luck, because P. J. Night has some more scares for you and your friends!

CREEPY CARNIVAL PUZZLER

Before things started getting creepy, Gabby and her friends were having a great time at the carnival! They each went on a ride and had a yummy carnival treat. Can you figure out what ride each friend went on and what treat he or she ate? Here's a hint to get started: Sydney ate a big bag of popcorn.

There are five clues below. Use this chart to record facts as you figure them out. Put an X in a box if you can rule it out. Use an O if it's a match.

CLUES

1. The boy who ordered cotton candy did not go on the merry-go-round.
2. The person who went on the roller coaster had funnel cake.
3. Austin's favorite ride is the Ferris wheel.

4. Sydney rode the merry-go-round. She wanted Gabby to come with her, but Gabby went on a ride with really big drops instead.

5. Tyler hates funnel cake and ice cream.

	Ferris Wheel	Tilt-a-whirl	Roller Coaster	Merry-Go-Round	Popcorn	Cotton Candy	Ice Cream	Funnel Cake
Gabby					X			
Sydney					O	X	X	X
Austin					X			
Tyler					X			
Popcorn								
Cotton Candy								
Ice Cream								
Funnel Cake								

YOU'RE INVITED TO . . .
CREATE YOUR OWN SCARY STORY!

Do you want to turn your sleepover into a creepover? Telling a spooky story is a great way to set the mood. P. J. Night has written a few sentences to get you started. Fill in the rest of the story and have fun scaring your friends.

You can also collaborate with your friends on this story by taking turns. Have everyone at your sleepover sit in a circle. Pick one person to start. She will add a sentence or two to the story, cover what she wrote with a piece of paper leaving only the last word or phrase visible, and then pass the story to the next girl. Once everyone has taken a turn, read the scary story you created together aloud!

As I walked into the fun house I felt the air getting colder and noticed the lights getting dimmer. I turned around to ask my friends if they felt this too, but they weren't behind me anymore—they must not have followed me into the fun house. I was trying to decide whether or not to keep going when all of a sudden the floor began moving beneath my feet. I was moved slowly in a circle until the floor stopped in front of a big black door. I turned the knob to open the door and . . .

_____

_____

_____

_____

_____

_____

_____

_____

_____

_____

_____

_____

_____

_____

THE END

A lifelong night owl, **P. J. NIGHT** often works furiously into the wee hours of the morning, writing down spooky tales and dreaming up new stories of the supernatural and otherworldly. Although P. J.'s whereabouts are unknown at this time, we suspect the author lives in a drafty, old mansion where the floorboards creak when no one is there and the flickering candlelight creates shadows that creep along the walls. We truly wish we could tell you more, but we've been sworn to keep P. J.'s identity a secret . . . and it's a secret we will take to our graves!

THE END

You're invited to a

If you like CREEPOVER

books, then you'll love

SARANORMAL

Available at your
favorite store

Saranormalbooks.com

Looking for another great book?
Find it in the middle.

in
the
middle
BOOKS

Fun, fantastic books for kids
in the in-beTWEEN age.

IntheMiddleBooks.com

SIMON & SCHUSTER
Children's Publishing

 /SimonKids